Rick Regan

The Webster Trilogy

Becoming the Widow Riley, 2021
The Daughter Problem, 2020
Art School Drama, 2022

The Webster Trilogy, by Rick Regan

Copyright 2023,

All rights reserved.

ISBN: 9798863627601
Imprint: Independently published

Independently published by the Author on Amazon.com

For information, please contact:

Rick Regan
PO Box 40039
Raleigh, NC 27629
rick@rickregan.net

Disclaimer

This is a work of fiction. Names, characters, businesses, places, events, and incidents are either the products of the author's imagination or used in a fictitious manner. Any resemblance to actual persons, living or dead, or actual events is purely coincidental.

Cover art by Maggie Loftus, Evanston, IL 2021, "Red Birds"

Contents

Introduction

This collection of plays is the story of families, in three different times and three different places.

<u>Becoming the Widow Riley</u> introduces Brigitte Sullivan as an about-to-graduate-from-college woman, in the middle of America's preparation for WWII. She is Eastern, Northern and from a *good family* in Rhode Island. When she falls in love with a sailor from Montana, her life starts to pick up speed, sending her ultimately to Montana. Along the way, there is a shift in the atmosphere, from sunny spring in Newport, RI, to the dark war concerns across the country, and finally the spare isolation of the Great Plains. Brigitte transforms herself from being a flighty schoolgirl to a mature adult woman. Her relationships and interactions with other women are the mileposts along the way for her maturity. The professor's lecture at the very beginning gives an outline of the new ideas about independence for Brigitte.

In <u>The Daughter Problem</u>, Wayne Webster is raising three daughters on a farm in northeast Montana in the mid-1950's. His wife Irine was killed in an ice-skating accident with her twin sister Coleen. At the beginning, Wayne and his brother Rueben are discussing how Coleen's husband Keme was also killed in an auto accident, leaving their daughter Josephine as an orphan. Wayne has taken Josephine in with his two daughters, Marie and Maeve. There is planning underway for an eighteenth birthday party for Josephine coming up. Oddly, the ghost of Irene is haunting Wayne's dreams at night. At the party we learn that the oldest daughter, Marie, may be in the *family-way* by her boyfriend, a local Native Ben Hair. Wayne recruits a local woman from town, the Widow (Brigitte) Riley, to come to the party to meet his bachelor brother Rueben. She quickly grasps the situation and gets things moving.

There is a lot going on in the Webster household and for Wayne, a widower and straight-arrow Montana grain farmer, all these women around create a wonderful, problematic chaos. And he loves it.

In <u>Art School Drama</u>, we follow the middle daughter Josephine to art school in Montreal in 1960. It is an election year in Quebec and the dynamic young candidate for Prime Minister, Jean Lesage, is a Kennedy-esque figure who hovers over the story. He comes to Montreal to make a speech and dazzles the crowd with rousing appeal to vote for change in the sclerotic Church-dominated French bureaucracy of Quebec at the time. Josephine is finishing art school and, as an American, the politics are mostly theoretical, but the speech does expose the political divide between herself and her boyfriend Otto. Just in time, she falls in with a cadre of French speaking leftist student organizers, who expose the hypocrisy the current state of affairs, as well as their more open attitudes around romance and relationships. Through it all she is trying to finish her art project and graduate, under the watchful eye of the head of the school, Gerard Fontainebleau. Like the Lesage's program of changes in Quebec, called the Quiet Revolution, Josephine is optimistic and hopeful about a bright new future.

Put together for the first time in this volume, The Webster Trilogy is oddly misnamed. The widow Brigitte Riley is of course not a Webster, yet. And Josephine's father was full-blood Blackfoot native, of the Assine tribe, but she takes Wayne Webster's name. Though she is probably not aware of it, she is probably passing as a Webster because that name would be common in Canada. I wonder if she would take up her native name later in life as an artist. We'll see!

BECOMING THE WIDOW RILEY

RICK REGAN

2022

<u>SCHOOL DAYS IN RHODE ISLAND</u>

I/E. SALVE REGINA COLLEGE CAMPUS - DAY

Early spring 1944 in Newport, Rhode Island. Nearing the end of term, the young women carry books to class along leafy sidewalks. The day is a bright, sunny New England spring morning.

Brigitte Sullivan is a smart, funny and popular student, walking with her friends to class. They enter a lecture hall and sit.

Classic lecture room with big blackboards, a podium in front and stadium-style seating. The room is about half full for the spring semester of "Shakespeare and You". The Professor is Dr. Marianne Bernstein, noted scholar and research academic. A Jew, she fled her university in Munich as the tensions in Germany grew ever more dangerous. She far outclasses the typically-average faculty at this small Catholic women's' college but she brings a European academic sophistication to this corner of America.

BERNSTEIN
(enters)
Gut morning, ladies. It is a pleasure on such a beautiful day to have you all here. Looking out I see that you are like a field of blooming flowers, fresh in the spring.
(general laughter)
Ah, yes. Now then, we take up where we left off, at the end of our love story, Romeo and Juliet.

The students open their books, ruffle pages. Brigitte Sullivan has her notes ready and a sharp pencil.

BERNSTEIN
I wish to begin this morning by examining our story through a lens of economics, particularly female economics. Our old friend Karl Marx tells us that we must understand the "Means of Production" and look closely at who "owns" the Means of Production.

We have here the story of two feuding families, wealthy, aristocratic, important families. These are not simple peasants out in the villages. They are not the kings either, yet they are closer to royalty than poverty. And daughters, you know, will produce grandchildren, but

they must be tightly controlled for the dynasty to continue. The stakes are very high indeed. And for Capulets to marry a Montague, is verboten!
(chuckles)
So here is our darling Juliet, the product of the Capulet dynasty. She is woo-ed my Mister Romantic himself, Romeo!

But look closely: she is the machine, the factory, the means of production - for grandchildren. So, Karl would ask, who controls the means of production? Her parents - oh, let's not kid ourselves - the father! Or she herself? This is the central question of the play: who gets to control Juliet?

And if the family cannot control Juliet, then she must die, because if the Capulets do not get the benefit of her production, her children, then no one will, especially the hated Montagues.

We see BRIGITTE writing.

BERNSTEIN
So I come back and ask you to consider: Is this then really a love story? Eh?! You can decide for yourself and explain it all to me - in your exam paper in two weeks.

And I must ask you the same thing, my flowers of spring, who controls you? Your parents? Your boyfriend? Or you yourself?

That's enough for today. Remember that exams will be in this room. The specific day and time will be posted. Thank you.

Dr. Bernstein gathers her materials and exits.

Brigitte Sullivan has written in her notes: Marry for love or money? Who controls you?

INT. THE BREAKERS (MANSION), NEWPORT, R.I - EVENING

Gladys Vanderbilt has opened the house to the Newport Society for social events as the War ramps up. Tonight the Naval Officer Candidates and NCO's are invited. The women of Salve Regina College, very near the mansion, are encouraged to attend and entertain the soldiers. There is music and punch, with tables set up inside and outside, and people can stroll along the lawn down to the water. Lovely spring evening.

There are already uniformed men and lots of young women, all mixing and mingling before the music gets going.

The commanding officer of the War College has been invited by Ms. Vanderbilt. He is Commander Tom Sterling. A sergeant follows the commander. They enter the room.

SERGEANT
(shouting)
A-TEN-TION!

All the sailors spin around, gawking at seeing such a high-ranking officer here, and become ram-rod stiff, at Attention. The women are silent and motionless.

STERLING
Now, boys. I think it's a great thing that Ms. Vanderbilt has offered her house for this evening's social event. She has very graciously invited us to enjoy this fine property. And, men!, are we thankful?!

ALL
YES SIR!

STERLING
And what do we say to Ms. Vanderbilt?

ALL
THANK YOU, MISS VANDERBILT!

STERLING
Very good. Now, listen to me men, Ms. Vanderbilt has a lovely house here. And I don't want to hear about any rough-housing or horseplay. If a single champagne flute is broken, you will all be peeling potatoes for a month. Behave yourselves and enjoy the party. Do - you - understand - me?!

ALL
YES, SIR!

STERLING
Very good. You are men of the United States Navy. Remember that!

That is all.

SERGEANT
(shouting)
As you were!

Sterling and the Sergeant are warmly greeted by Ms. Vanderbilt and her attendants. They all exit out to the verandah overlooking the seaside.

The band strikes up a tune and people move to the dance floor.

INT. LARGE BATHROOM IN THE MANSION - SAME TIME

Close up on a box of matches. A woman's hand with shiny red nails picks up the box, pulls out a match and strikes it on the side, flaring the match. We see her light a cigarette and see the mirror is crowded with women working on touch ups.

Brigitte Sullivan is brushing her eyebrows. Her friend Maggie is with her.

MAGGIE
You look very nice tonight, BRIGITTE.

BRIGITTE
Thanks, Mags. You too. I'm sure every sailor in the room will want a dance with you.

MAGGIE
More than that, I hope!

NANCY
You better strike while the iron's hot then. You *Salve?*

MAGGIE
Excuse me?

NANCY
You heard me. I'm Nancy. I graduated last year from Salve Regina. So let me give you some advice. There will be upward of one-

hundred-and-fifty women here tonight, all looking to land a Navy man. But there are only seventy or eighty sailor-boys, at my last count. You know what that means? When you find a good one, you better set your harpoon and reel him in - before he gets away.

BRIGITTE
That's a funny way to look at it. Usually, it's the fellas that are chasing the girls.

NANCY
Not tonight, honey. Tonight, you have access to the finest selection of American men anywhere. It should be shooting fish in a barrel to pick out the one you like. But oh no! It's a feeding frenzy all right. Gals from Providence, Boston, New Haven, there is even a train from New York City. These are women who act fast, know the game and play sharp elbows.

MAGGIE
So, what do we do?

NANCY
Do you have a strategy?

BRIGITTE
Strategy?

NANCY
You have to have a plan, you ducks! Here's my plan: I find a good looking fella, wheel him out for a dance, and if he's not too handsy, or maybe if he is, I direct him out to the lawn, where we can be alone, or at least out of reach of the claws and hooks of the husband-seeking hoards inside. I take him for a test drive - with a kiss - and see how it goes. If he's a dead fish, I cut him loose and go back to the arena of gladiators. But if it works out, well, I have my eye on a little house on the Cape for our first place. Our cozy love nest by the sea.

BRIGITTE
But aren't they going to the war?

NANCY
That's why we gotta act fast. Don't get left behind or you'll get run over.

(stubs out the cigarette)
See you duckys in the funny papers.

NANCY exits. BRIGITTE finishes her touch up and Maggie looks at her.

MAGGIE
I guess this will have to do.

BRIGITTE
You look great. Let's go!

They weave through the other women primping and emerge into a large ornate ballroom. The music is going, and people are dancing. There are people moving around everywhere and it is hard to know where to go.

MAGGIE
(loudly)
I think there is punch on the other side. I'll go get some.

BRIGITTE
You go. I'm going to look around.

MAGGIE
Happy hunting!

Maggie disappears into the swirl of people.

BRIGITTE sees an open corner where there is some space to breathe. She moves through the throng of uniformed men and glamorous women. She realizes that she looks pretty ordinary and simple compared to these women with tall heels, brassy hair in swoops, gold earrings and plum lipstick and eyeshadow. She passes a bronze mirror on the wall, and she sees herself, looking like a Catholic schoolgirl. She sighs.

She looks up and sees a tall man in uniform. He is lanky and seems shy, maybe awkward. She looks, thinks of the NANCY, and steps forward.

BRIGITTE
You not dancing? Plenty of women for dancing.

CHARLEY
Oh, yeah. These gals are fine looking but quite out of my league.

BRIGITTE

Your league?

CHARLEY
I'm still pitching in minors, you know.

BRIGITTE
You talk funny. You from around here?

CHARLEY
Oh, no. I'm a long way from home.

BRIGITTE
Well.... If you don't want to dance, could we take a walk outside, see the ocean?

CHARLEY
That could be nice.

BRIGITTE
Nice night.

CHARLEY
Well then, lead the way.

BRIGITTE
(to herself)
Oh no, you're not giving me the slip...
(to Charley)
There are so many people, I'd rather follow you. That way.

Charley and BRIGITTE move through the crowd toward the door. The NANCY catches BRIGITTE's eye, dancing mid-dip. She sees Charley and winks at BRIGITTE.

Quickly another uniformed man grabs BRIGITTE's hand and reels her in, spinning her around and holding her for a dance.

BUCK
Hi, I'm Buck!

BRIGITTE
Buck?

BUCK

That's what they call me, Buck. Let's dance!

He begins spinning her around and dipping her.

BRIGITTE
But I...!

BUCK
Don't worry, darling. You're in good hands with the Buckaroo!

They dance and move further away from the door. Charley is gone, out of sight.

BRIGITTE
(to herself)
Sometimes they get away.

BUCK
What's that?

BRIGITTE
You a flyboy, Buck?

BUCK
Nah, been on the water since I was a pup. I'm an old water dog. Boats it is for me!

They get to the edge of the dancing and stop for a breath.

Buck pulls out a small flask and grabs a quick sip.

BRIGITTE
What's that?

BUCK
Brandy. Ever have any? Keeps the chill out, on cold nights, like tonight. Keeps ya' warm. Want some?

BRIGITTE
No thanks!

BUCK
Aw don't be a spoil. Be a sport! Come on.

He *pushes the flask to her.*

BRIGITTE
Gotta live, I guess.

She takes the flask, has a sip and grimaces.

*B*UCK
Smooth, huh?

BRIGITTE
Too much! Oh my.

BUCK
Listen, doll, you want to take a walk in the moonlight? Maybe we find a nice hideaway for an evening of...?

BRIGITTE
Socializing? I don't think that's what you've got in mind. But let me introduce you to my pal, Mags. She's a great sport!

*M*aggie *is passing by, following a fellow. BRIGITTE grabs her and spins her toward Buck.*

MAGGIE
BRIGITTE!

BRIGITTE
Maggie, meet my friend Buck. He's a barrel of laughs.

MAGGIE
Is that right?

BUCK
Oh yeah! I'm a ton of fun. Want to dance?

MAGGIE
(to BRIGITTE)
Did I see you with a pocket rocket?

BRIGITTE
A what? Oh! Yeah, Buck, give Mags here a taste.

BUCK

Coming right up!

He pulls out the flask and BRIGITTE takes a pull.

MAGGIE
Whew! Now we've got a party. Come on!

She grabs Buck and they swing into the next dance.

BRIGITTE steams toward the door. Outside she finds couples embracing and strolling together. She's lost him.

BRIGITTE
Oh, shoot!

Charley is behind her, out of sight, leaning against the wall casually.

CHARLEY
You lose something?

BRIGITTE
(spins)
Oh! There you are. I thought you were gone.

CHARLEY
Like I said, these gals are out of my league. I just figured you were one of 'em and got a better offer. Nice night though, you're right.

BRIGITTE
Let's walk.

They stroll the grounds in the moonlight. Water laps at the edge of the lawn, at the breakwater.

CHARLEY
So how is it you come to be here tonight? All these gals seem to be hunting for a fella. Nice girl like you shouldn't have any trouble in that department.

BRIGITTE
You're sweet.

CHARLEY
Oh, I doubt it. But no fella for you?

BRIGITTE
I'm still in school and we don't get much chance to socialize.

CHARLEY
(alarmed)
Still in school? Well, now listen, I'd better be getting you back. Wouldn't want to get you in trouble.

He moves quickly to head back to the mansion.

BRIGITTE
No, no! It's not like that. I'm about to graduate. Salve Regina, it's right next door. You can practically see it from here.

CHARLEY
That's college?

BRIGITTE
Right. Yes. For women.

CHARLEY
Well now. Puts a different shape to it.

BRIGITTE
Maybe you should kiss me.

CHARLEY
I suppose, in time that'd be the thing, but no hurry about that. I've not much practice, you see.

BRIGITTE
Well, I'm here. You're here. The moon's out. We could... practice, together. If you'd like.

CHARLEY
Well now, I'd say you're about the prettiest thing I've seen out here. Might be that kissing you would be the right thing to do. But, I say, Ol' Charley, give her a think before you leap. Let's consider the matter a moment.

BRIGITTE
You don't want to kiss me, is that it? I guess there are some fellows inside that might be interested.

CHARLEY
Oh now, I know you'd have a lot of takers. I've been training with these fellows for months, boys from all over, even from down south. And I'd be hard pressed to find a group of men as desperate for some kisses and home cooking. I get feeling blue myself sometimes, thinking about women and such. Kind of a puzzle for most men, I guess.

BRIGITTE
A puzzle? Women? We're just regular people, just like you all.

CHARLEY
Sure, that'd be right. Yep. Same as, same as. I've got to remember that.

They come to an unoccupied bench, conveniently overlooking the harbor opening and out to the Atlantic Ocean. They sit.

BRIGITTE
What do you mean, you feel blue? About what?

CHARLEY
I suppose that's a kind of a long story and maybe we don't have time for that.

BRIGITTE
Since we're not going to p*ractice,* I guess we have time. Go ahead.

CHARLEY
Well, when a fellow gets to thinking about things, it's like one thing builds on another. Think about what I want, what I've seen others do and go through, and what with the war and all, seems like a question of which way the wind is blowing, and am I walking into it or being blown by it? Hard to make out. And the big things, like Uncle Sam, come a-knocking and a fellow doesn't seem to have much choice anyhow. And maybe that's for the best, sometimes I think. Sometimes to get in the great stream of events and history and the like, we have to get in the wind and get blown along for a-ways, like the tumbleweed. You end up someplace different but maybe you didn't even know you needed to go there. Like here. Like right now. Why as I turn it over, I see that you are right, again. I should kiss you because the whole world might be depending on it. Probably is, and look at me staring at my shoes. Perhaps we should begin.

17

She stares at him. He is motionless. Finally, she leans in and kisses him, his mouth closed and eyes open. She is not much better but has seen movies and knows that the woman is supposed to put her head back and close her eyes. He has not seen these movies and is confused.

BRIGITTE
How was that?

CHARLEY
Real nice. Like I said, I don't have much practice.

BRIGITTE
Let's try again. But this time, maybe close your eyes, relax your mouth and, I guess, put your arms around me, for a minute or so.

CHARLEY
OK. We'll try her out.

Charley clamps his eyes closed, waggles his jaw and puts his arms straight out. BRIGITTE, seeing this, snuggles forward and pushes herself up against his body. They kiss and he holds her.

BRIGITTE
That's better.

CHARLEY
You are very pretty.

BRIGITTE
Thank you. You're a tall drink of water, yourself. Where are you from anyway?

CHARLEY
Down by way of Montana. Tucked up in the corner by Canada and Dakota. Just off the rez.

BRIGITTE
The rez?

CHARLEY
Bureau of Indian Affairs has a reservation in those parts. Blackfeet

mostly.

BRIGITTE
Are you Indian?

CHARLEY
No, I don't believe the Riley's have any Indian blood.

BRIGITTE
Riley? Irish?

CHARLEY
Charles Riley, Medicine Lake, Montana. Pleased to meet you.

BRIGITTE
The pleasure is all mine. Brigitte Sullivan, of Providence, Rhode Island.

CHARLEY
Well don't that beat it. A Riley and a Sullivan.

BRIGITTE
Just chance, I guess. What did you do in Medicine Lake?

CHARLEY
I grew up there but went over to Helena for college. Just got out myself.

BRIGITTE
For navy, sailing things?

CHARLEY
Oh no. A writer's program. My old man ran one of the mines up there. He went to miners' college himself, wanted me to as well. But I finished school and wanted to play baseball. I was on the minor league team nearby and we travelled all summer. One of the coaches was a reporter for a newspaper and had me read some of his stuff. Then he asked me to write a few things about being on the team, the season and baseball in general. He liked them and sometimes turned them in to his paper, under his name.

BRIGITTE
But that's not right!

CHARLEY
No, no! He was showing me that my stuff was good enough to print, good enough for the paper. I saved some of the clippings.

BRIGITTE
Still, that doesn't seem right.

CHARLEY
He encouraged me and pointed me to a writer's program at Tech. He said I'd have a lot longer career as a journalist than a pitcher in the minors, or at least get paid better. So I went. But along the way I read the novels and poems, about the Great War you see. How it was like a big machine just grinding up and killing a whole generation of young men. And I thought that with the new war on, I'd be a reporter and write about the fighting from eye-level.

BRIGITTE
So, you're not a sailor?

CHARLEY
Oh, I'm a qualified seaman, first class. But I am trying to get hitched onto the intelligence branch. But first is to get through the sailor training.

BRIGITTE
What do you want to do when you get out?

CHARLEY
If I make it back, I guess I'll go back and look after my mother in Montana. And maybe write a book about my experience in war. That's about as far as I've got.

BRIGITTE
What about a wife? A family?

CHARLEY
Hmmm... well, yeah, I guess so. That's what a fella does. But hasn't been much of an opportunity for that.

BRIGITTE
There aren't any pretty girls in Montana?

CHARLEY
Oh boy-howdy! Prettiest you ever seen, or at least I've ever seen. I mean, until now. Until seeing you.

BRIGITTE
Don't you want to get married and have a family?

CHARLEY
I hadn't really given it too much thought, until now you mention it. You wouldn't want to get married, would you?

BRIGITTE
Well, this is quite sudden, but I would entertain it. Are you proposing?

CHARLEY
Here? Now?

BRIGITTE
It is quite a romantic spot. Seems as nice a place as a woman would want to get a proposal.

CHARLEY
Well, all right. Miss Sullivan, would you marry me?

BRIGITTE
Thank you for your kind offer, Mister Riley but I barely know you. Perhaps we could meet again, tomorrow, and consider the matter again. Do you have a car?

CHARLEY
Um, yep.

BRIGITTE
Then pick me up tomorrow at noon, at the front of Salve Regina. If we leave now, you can take me, I will be in before curfew.

CHARLEY
It's a plan then.

Charley moves to get up.

BRIGITTE
Charley?

CHARLEY
Miss Sullivan?

BRIGITTE
Let's practice one more time, just to see if it is working alright.

She snuggles in again and they kiss a long time.

CHARLEY
Oh my, you are the real, flesh-and-blood item.

BRIGITTE
Just a regular person, just like you.

CHARLEY
That's right, same-as, same-as.

They get up and walk back to the house. They get to his car and drive back to her school. They kiss and she gets out.

BRIGITTE
Tomorrow then. Noon?

CHARLEY
Yes, Sir!

She goes in and he drives away.

EXT. NEWPORT, R.I. - DAY

Charley arrives to pick up Brigitte. The morning has gotten cloudy and started to drizzle. Charley is in his 'casual' uniform. BRIGITTE is slightly overdressed in a skirt and sweater top.

CHARLEY
Hello Miss Sullivan.

BRIGITTE
Good afternoon, Mister Riley. Shall we go for a drive?

CHARLEY
Yes, please.

She gets in and they drive in silence for a way. They cruise along the Easton Bay road. At an overlook with parking, Charley parks the car, wipers still sweeping the windscreen. He turns the car off and they sit quietly. The rain is starting to really drum on the roof of the car.

BRIGITTE
Quite wet today.

CHARLEY
Yeah, it's what they forecast.

BRIGITTE
Mister Riley.

CHARLEY
Miss Sullivan.

BRIGITTE
Mister Riley, I think we should probably start again.

CHARLEY
I see. Which part do you want to back up to, the one where you lose me in the crowd?

BRIGITTE
No. What I mean is that I spoke too quickly last night. I shouldn't have pressed you into saying anything about getting married. I have exams in another week and I have to finish school.

CHARLEY
You've had some time to think it over, I see.

BRIGITTE
Yes, and I think I was too hasty. Don't you?

CHARLEY
Well, when you say it like that, it does seem quick.

BRIGITTE
So, maybe you should just take me back.

CHARLEY
I can do that if you like but...

BRIGITTE
Yes, it's a miserable day, all this rain.

CHARLEY
But...

BRIGITTE
I mean, you don't even know me. I can be a mean person. There are times that my mother and I have fights. My friends wonder why I'm reading all the time instead of going out with the boys, like a normal person. I'm kind of a mess and it's just not fair to you. You seem like a nice guy and I'm sure there will be plenty of actually stable and functioning girls that will throw themselves at you. Do you understand, at all? Or am I just making this worse? Oh, I've been thinking about it all night. Thinking about Juliet and Jane Austen, and all of the women who get married, even when they are not in love, and I get confused because maybe I am in love. I don't know what to do. Do you? Am I messing it all up?
(starts crying)
I'm sorry! I shouldn't be crying. I said I wouldn't cry! But you were so nice to me, and I just got so caught up.

CHARLEY
(chuckling)
Hey, hey, now, simmer down. It's alright. You're not messing anything up. I was thinking about you all night too. Maybe our spirits got tangled up in the night air. It happens. It's alright.

BRIGITTE
So, okay. Maybe you should just take me back.

CHARLEY
Alright, I'll do that. But there is one thing I was thinking about.

BRIGITTE
What's that?

CHARLEY

Well, I don't know right much about houses and neighborhoods. And I'm coming up on finishing my training and qualify to live off-base. I wasn't going to fool with it, but now you got me thinking. And I'm looking around at these houses and I don't know which one to pick. What makes a good house?

BRIGITTE
(sensibly)
Well, a good house has a solid foundation, just like people. And good light. Nice high ceilings are good. Plenty of room for a bed and a table. Some kitchen things. That sort of thing.

CHARLEY
Maybe on the ways back you could point out a couple that catch your eye.

BRIGITTE
Well, alright. I'm always glad to be a help.

CHARLEY
Sure, sure. And one other thing. I went to see a fellow this morning, on a buddy's recommendation, and I picked up something for you.

Charley fishes in his pocket and pulls out a small velvet bag with a tie at the top.

BRIGITTE
Charley? What's this?

CHARLEY
I suppose you could call it a good-luck charm, for your exams and such.

She opens the satchel and pulls out a solid gold ring. It is heavy, like a man's ring but sized for a smaller hand.

BRIGITTE
Oh my!

CHARLEY
Now look here. You've got some things to settle. I do as well. I'd like you to hang onto that for a while, through your exams and such. Then, when you have a few minutes, we could see about whether we

should visit a priest, or a judge and the like. But you get to decide, keep the ring anyhow, either way. I think of it like a deposit, and if things don't work out, you keep it. But take some time and decide for yourself. I realized you are just too valuable to let slip away. I'd regret it my whole life if I missed a chance with you.

BRIGITTE
Oh, Charley.

CHARLEY
A buddy of mine says, some people climb mountains, and that's something, but finding somebody that you love and care about, that's real achievement. So, just put that back in that little sack and put it in your pocket. If you want to wear it, that's up to you.

BRIGITTE
Skirts don't have pockets.

CHARLEY
My mother's did. She sews 'em on. Real handy.

BRIGITTE
I'll remember that when I meet her.

CHARLEY
Won't that be something?

BRIGITTE
(exhales)
Oh my. Okay. Let's go back.

They start driving again.

CHARLEY
Keep your eyes peeled along here. I was thinking that a water view might be nice. Any of these strike your fancy?

BRIGITTE
Go down that street. That one is pretty.

CHARLEY
You like that one?

BRIGITTE
It alright. Go down that way, turn up the street there.

CHARLEY
Alright.

They drive along through neighborhoods, rambling around in the rain.

INT. SALVE REGINA COLLEGE CAMPUS - MORNING

The classroom of Professor Bernstein's exam. The students are all in place. BRIGITTE is there with her workbook and pencil.

MAGGIE
(whispers)
Brige! Brige.

BRIGITTE
What Mags?! We're about to start.

MAGGIE
Is that what I think it is? A ring?

BRIGITTE
It's a good luck charm, from a friend.

MAGGIE
Sure it is. Are you pregnant already?

BRIGITTE
Mag! No. No, I am not pregnant. Are you?

MAGGIE
I don't think so, but I have to stay away from Buck for a while. It's getting too hot and heavy.

BRIGITTE
Jesus, Mags, what's got into you?

MAGGIE
Like she said, set the hook and reel 'em in, before they get away.

BRIGITTE
Just focus, for today, focus.

MAGGIE
Right.

The exam papers come around and the clock ticks down. At the end of the time the proctor calls time and they put pencils down and turn in the exams.

EXT. SALVE REGINA COLLEGE CAMPUS - DAY - GRADUATION DAY

Brigitte and Maggie stand around with a group of friends, wearing mortar boards and graduation gowns. Parents sit at picnic tables nearby in the grass. Everyone is celebrating. ASTRID's mother is chatting with the other parents.

MAGGIE
I can't believe we made it. Did you see Professor Bernstein's face when she handed out the diplomas?

BRIGITTE
She was so happy for everybody.

They sip champagne together and toast each other and all they have been through during the four years.

MAGGIE
I guess we have to start our lives now. What's next, do you know?

BRIGITTE
Are you and Buck going to get married?

MAGGIE
I don't know. They are all going to be shipped out, when the war really gets going. I don't want to be a widow at twenty-one. Do you?

BRIGITTE
Well, no, of course not. But Charley is trying to get signed up on the intelligence group, to be a reporter, not shooting at people. So, I think he will be safer, don't you?

MAGGIE
Maybe. But you think you'll get married? You've been wearing that ring out!

BRIGITTE
I want to talk to my mother about it, see if she thinks it's a good idea.

MAGGIE

But don't you make your own decisions? Love or money, right?

BRIGITTE
Somebody just finished their exams!

MAGGIE
Ha! Brige, just follow your heart, alright.

BRIGITTE
You too, Mags. If the Buckaroo is right for you, you know the way to the altar.

MAGGIE
Awww, I'm going to miss you, Brige. We had so much fun. But it's like, we have to start our lives now. Do you want to get a job?

BRIGITTE
I want to have my own money, that's one thing I learned from my mother. She worked on-and-off all during my growing up and let me tell you, she was a lot happier when she had a job and made her own way.

MAGGIE
I don't want to live like a spinster though. Maybe we could get an apartment up in Providence and look for jobs. We could even split a car.

BRIGITTE
What would I tell Charles?

MAGGIE
That you want to live your own life. Being married to a sailor is hardly being married at all, what with getting shipped off to who knows where. Think of it, Brige, we can make our own way in the world, like we always talked about. And travel, see some of the world. Read novels and write poetry. We can be our own women.

BRIGITTE
But I'll lose Charley. I don't think I could bear to lose him now. He's different than the other boys. He is thoughtful and respects me. He's not all grabby like the college boys. I think I love him.

MAGGIE

Becoming the Widow Riley

You can love him when he gets back.

BRIGITTE
But I want to love him now.

MAGGIE
(long pause)
Then I guess you've made up your mind.

BRIGITTE
I guess so. I didn't really know it until I said it out loud.

MAGGIE
Then, Brige, I wish you and your Charley all the love in the world!

They hug.

BRIGITTE
Thanks, Mags. And if it works out with you and the Buckaroo, then I hope you are both happy too. Now, let's just celebrate the day.

MAGGIE
Cheers, girl!

BRIGITTE
Cheers!

They raise their glasses.

INT. DINNER AT RESTAURANT - EVENING

Brigitte is there with her mother, Astrid Sullivan. It is a dim and cozy restaurant and the two sit across from each other, looking at the menus.

ASTRID
What are you having?

BRIGITTE
Just a salad, I think. How about you?

ASTRID
Oysters! And champagne. It's a celebration and that always means

oysters for me. And what's better with oysters than champagne?

BRIGITTE
A gin Gimlet.

ASTRID
What? What did you say?

BRIGITTE
I said a gin Gimlet, to go with the oysters. Better than champagne, I think.

ASTRID
Well, now, aren't we the *connoisseur?* Where did you learn to drink pints of gin? Not at S*alve,* I'd bet.

BRIGITTE
Oh mother. It's just that when we would go out on the town and somebody started ordering cocktails, I couldn't think of anything or remember their names, but I could come up with 'gin Gimlet!' I don't even like them very much but it's easy to order.

ASTRID
I see. And the ring? I noticed, you know.

BRIGITTE
A friend gave it to me, as a good luck charm for my exams.

ASTRID
A friend? Right.

BRIGITTE
Yes, he's in the Navy.

ASTRID
Well, now, that is promising. What's his name?

BRIGITTE
Charles Riley.

ASTRID
Where is he from? Is he from Boston?

BRIGITTE

Montana.

ASTRID
Good lord, girl! You're mixing yourself up with a cowboy, in the Navy? No. This has to stop.

BRIGITTE
What? Why?

ASTRID
Take it off. Just take it off. That'll be the end of it. You can return it to him if it makes you feel better.

BRIGITTE
But I love him.

ASTRID
Ha! That old chestnut! Listen Bridge, you'll pack up your things and come back to Providence with me.

BRIGITTE
But I need a couple of days!

ASTRID
OK, I'll go home and come back for you at the end of the week.

BRIGITTE
I don't understand.

ASTRID
You are not going to go directly from school into a wedding with a dusty sailor. No, there are very good prospects in Providence, with bankers, insurance people, industrialists. I won't see your education wasted on some roustabout.

BRIGITTE
But I want to make up my own mind.

ASTRID
When you fall in love with a Rockefeller, you can make up your own mind. Until then, you're coming back to Providence.

BRIGITTE
But I'm a grown woman.

ASTRID
Listen, honey, I am very proud of you. You graduated, top of your class, and you made it through college. Now let's get you back to Providence, where we can get you on the social calendar, for the summer season.

BRIGITTE
But I don't want to go back to Providence.

ASTRID
That doesn't matter. You're coming back with me at the end of the week. That settles it. And take that damned ring off.

BRIGITTE
You haven't even met him. He's nice.

ASTRID
He could have come to the graduation today. Was he there, because I didn't get introduced.

BRIGITTE
No, he has training at the base.

A waiter asks about ordering.

ASTRID
Can you give us a few more minutes? No, wait. I'll have a vodka Martini and she wants a gin Gimlet. Thank you.

The waiter takes the order and goes away.

The two sit in silence for a minute and the waiter returns with their drinks.

BRIGITTE
Mother, I can't believe you came all this way, down to Newport, just to haul me back to Providence. I'm not a child.

ASTRID
Says the girl wearing an engagement ring. Hmm... perhaps you are right.

Astrid picks up the Martini glass and takes a long pull.

Brigitte sips the Gimlet.

BRIGITTE
What do you mean, I'm right?

ASTRID
So cold! Mmmmm! Ahem. Yes, perhaps I haven't been seeing along the right line. Maybe my work is done here. Get you married off to a sailor-boy, I don't have to worry about you anymore. Until the babies come, but that takes time.

BRIGITTE
Hmmm....

ASTRID
Or does it? Wait, are you already in the family way? Brigitte, how could you? You are a shameful girl, opening your thighs for the whole fleet t*o sail right up in! I* guess I expected too much of *Salve Regina,* to guard and protect my child from the grinning wolves gathered at the front gate. Oh, honey, how could you? How far along are you?

BRIGITTE
Mom! I'm not like that! I haven't done anything with Charley yet. He's nice to me. And he's really shy. Why, I even had to teach him how to kiss. Can you believe that?

ASTRID
Expert kissing lessons, from my painted-tart daughter? Do you know what a whore is? Do you?

BRIGITTE
Mother!

ASTRID
A whore is a woman who trades her body, access to her sex, for money. I guess a gold ring is enough to turn your head, eh Cleopatra?

BRIGITTE
Mother, I'm not like you. I am going to be my own woman. There is a lot going on in the world and I want to be in it. And that means I'm not coming back to Providence.

ASTRID
Oh, your rear-admiral in-tow is going to make a cozy love-nest for you here in Newport, is that it? Meanwhile he's probably got women all over town and a girl in every port. These sailor brag to each other about how they have families on every continent. You know that, don't you, that men are liars, cheaters and only want to use a girl like you for sport.

BRIGITTE
What do you mean, a girl like me? Do you even know me?

ASTRID
Look, we'll make this all go away back in Providence. Give the boy his ring back, pack up your stuff, and I'll pick you up on Friday. Alright?

Brigitte gets up.

ASTRID
Where are you going?

BRIGITTE
I'm not hungry.

ASTRID
Just sit down.

BRIGITTE
I'm not going to sit here and listen to you call me nasty names and boss me around like a schoolgirl. I'm going back to my room.

ASTRID
Brigitte! Sit down, now!

BRIGITTE
Goodbye mother. Have a safe trip back home.

Brigitte stomps away.

ASTRID
Brigitte!

Astrid looks at the drinks on the table. She picks up the Martini and finishes it. Then she reaches across and takes the Gimlet. She sips it, nods, and downs the whole thing. She sets the glass down and sighs.

EXT. - EASTON BAY OVERLOOK - MID-MORNING - THE NEXT DAY

Charley and BRIGITTE sit on the bench at the overlook, surveying the water. The day is bright and getting warmer.

CHARLEY
Miss Sullivan.

BRIGITTE
Mister Riley.

CHARLEY
I see you are wearing your good luck charm. I trust it was helpful.

BRIGITTE
It certainly got my mother's attention.

CHARLEY
Was she happy?

BRIGITTE
Over the moon! She said, m*y work is done!*

CHARLEY
How's that?

BRIGITTE
By getting me married, she is happy to just pawn me off to somebody else. I told her I want to be my own woman, make my own life. But she just laughed.

CHARLEY
Be your own woman? Is that right?

BRIGITTE
Don't tell me you have old-fashioned views on the topic? Can't a

woman make her own way in the world? Is that what you're saying, that you want me to be the little housewife who sweeps and cooks and cleans up after you, like a little boy? Well, I didn't graduate *cum laude t*o stay home and be a nursemaid to a boy still wet behind the ears! You can get that idea right out of your head.

CHARLEY
Alright.

BRIGITTE
I mean it's a modern world. Women are working in all kinds of places now, even factories and mines. Women do all sorts of things these days.

CHARLEY
You want to take up mining?

BRIGITTE
No, of course I don't want to take up mining. I don't know the first thing about mining. Why would you say a thing like that?

CHARLEY
Oh, no reason.

BRIGITTE
No, the thing is, Charley. Well, here's the thing, the main thing. My friend Maggie wants me to get an apartment with her up in Providence and get jobs. You see a girl has to stand on her own two feet. You see what I mean?

CHARLEY
Yep. I suppose I do.

BRIGITTE
But I told her, just yesterday really, that the whole wide world isn't exactly waiting for two new college graduates to come out and set the world on fire. The world will spin just fine on its own. And it's not like there is a whole lot that's interesting to do in Providence anyhow. Does that make any sense?

CHARLEY
Yeah. Real clear.

BRIGITTE
So, as you can see, I think it's time you made your intentions plain. What do you have in mind to do with me and when are you going to start? That's the main thing, really, in a nutshell. I just think it's a dreadful thing to do to tell a woman that you are thinking of marrying to forget about her life and work and making her own money. It's just cruel, if you ask me, and I wonder where you get the nerve to say such things, to ME of all people. So, Mister, I think you need to level your wings and fly right, that's all.

CHARLEY
You sure that's all?

BRIGITTE
Oh, come now! Don't start lecturing me about how to behave as woman and a wife. Wait until you have to dance backwards in high-heels, with some pawing frat-boy swinging you around like a beer keg. Until you've experienced what it means to be a female, I mean REALLY experience it, you can hold your holier-than-thou sermons about the meaning of motherhood and apple pie. Apple Pie, if that's not a metaphor for something else, I don't know what is.

CHARLEY
You mean dessert, like with a cup of hot coffee?

BRIGITTE
No! Like Adam and Eve and the apple in the Garden of Eden, and Eve slicing it up and making a pie out of it. The homemaker serving up the fruit-of-knowledge, of death, of carnal knowledge and sin.

CHARLEY
I think you might have lost me on that one.

BRIGITTE
Well anyway, as I was saying, Mags wants to get an apartment together, but I told her I loved you.

CHARLEY
Well now.

BRIGITTE

And maybe we could get one of those houses down the street.

CHARLEY
That sounds nice.

BRIGITTE
And if we get married, maybe we could try to have a baby.

CHARLEY
That's a big step but I'd be willing.

BRIGITTE
To try?

CHARLEY
Might take a lot of practice.

BRIGITTE
A lot of trying.

CHARLEY
That would be something.

BRIGITTE
But, Charley, I'm not sure I even know who you are. It's all so fast. I don't know what you believe in.

CHARLEY
Me?

BRIGITTE
Yes, you!

CHARLEY
Well alright. I'll take a swing at it, but I don't know if I'll be able to loop in Adam and Eve, like you just did.

BRIGITTE
I'm sorry. Maybe that wasn't necessary.

CHARLEY
That's alright. Give me something to chew over at night.

BRIGITTE
But do you understand what I mean?

CHARLEY
Well, I'll tell you, Miss Sullivan. I go by a code, a kind of Prairie Philosophy. I find I need some ideas to ground myself to so that I stay steady when the wind gets too strong.

BRIGITTE
Like when?

CHARLEY
Like right now, with you.

BRIGITTE
Oh, no! Am I pushing you away, Charley?

CHARLEY
No, no. You're fine. It's just that out West, the wind doesn't care if it's blowing dust in your face. The snow and the rain are not concerned with the calf who falls into the creek. It takes the cow and the cowboy to go and look for that calf, notice that the little guy is missing and go out into the weather to fetch him.

BRIGITTE
So, self-reliance then.

CHARLEY
Not exactly. Let me try a baseball story. It takes others, you know. Throw the ball to the batter, swing at the pitch, field and throw to another base. You see, it takes others to make it in the world. Mother Nature is not going to look out for you, so we have to look out for each other.

BRIGITTE
So, we should work on things together.

CHARLEY
Well, more than that, because without a basic kindness and generosity, it's easy to think that striking it rich with an oil well means that I deserve to be rich. But it just means that we should share even more with our fellow cowboys.

BRIGITTE
But how can you be going to war? Won't you have to shoot people, the other soldiers?

CHARLEY
I'll do that if I have to but mostly I want to write down what I see, what I hear, understand what war is.

BRIGITTE
But what about me?

CHARLEY
Well Miss Sullivan, if you'll have me, would you marry me and be my bride?

BRIGITTE
Yes, Mister Riley. I will marry you.

CHARLEY
Best seal the deal with a kiss, wouldn't you say.

BRIGITTE
Yes, Mister Riley. Step right up!

They kiss in the bright sunlight.

CHARLEY
I guess we'd better get this train moving.

BRIGITTE
Oh, Charley, I'm so happy. I can't believe it's true.

CHARLEY
You've made me the happiest fella I know. Now let's get at her.

They get up and go to the car. They drive around looking at rental houses.

I/E. AROUND NEWPORT - VARIOUS TIMES

We see the couple signing paperwork at a city office, getting married.

We see the couple moving furniture around a small rental house.

We see the couple having dinner together in the new place.

We see the couple holding hands, next to each other in a small bed.

We see Charley swat his alarm clock and get up, get dressed and head to the base. She rests in bed, sprawled like a cat in the sheets.

We see the couple walking along the shore, holding hands in the evening.

INT. RILEY HOUSE - MORNING

In the bedroom, Charley is awake, staring at the ceiling. Next to him, BRIGITTE is also awake, staring at the ceiling.

On the bedside table an alarm clock rings.

BRRRAAAAAAANNNNNNGGGGGGG!

Charley swats it off. He sits at the side of the bed.

CHARLEY
Today's the day.

Brigitte hugs him from behind, holding him down.

BRIGITTE
Don't go, honey. You don't have to go. Just don't go.

CHARLEY
Old Uncle Sam would come looking for me. It's time.

He gets up and we see him lather his face, shave and splash water all around. He puts on his uniform and stands, looking at her. She is a mess, collapsing into tears.

BRIGITTE
Oh my god, Charley. I'm afraid this is the last time I will ever see you.

CHARLEY
Well then, best take a good look, Missus Riley. Take a good long look. That way you'll remember me when I come walking back up

that street.

BRIGITTE
Oh god, I can't believe you are going?

CHARLEY
Life of a sailor. Time to ship out. But I'll be alright. You just hang on to that good luck charm and I'll be back before you know it.

Charley gathers his navy duffle bag and heads to the front door.

*B*RIGITTE
I'm going to be all alone, Charley. What am I going to do without you?

CHARLEY
You'll be fine, dear. And we'll knock the stuffing out of them Gerrys, and they'll send us home by Christmas. But if it does take a while, check in on my mother for me, would you?

BRIGITTE
In Montana?

CHARLEY
Promise me that, please. That you'll look in on her.

BRIGITTE
OK, I promise, but I've never been to Montana.

CHARLEY
It's a big state. Hard to miss it once you are pointed that way.

BRIGITTE
I can't believe that you have to leave now.

CHARLEY
Kiss me and I have to go.

They kiss in a long embrace.

BRIGITTE
(crying)
Goodbye Charley.

CHARLEY
Goodbye Missus Riley. You hold tight. I won't be gone long.

He kisses her once more and goes out the door, walking down the street, duffel over his shoulder, to the bus stop around the corner. On the sidewalk are other sailors, all getting shipped out. They get on the bus and are gone.

THE OVERLAND WAY

I/E. ON THE TRAIN TO NEW YORK - DAY

We see Brigitte on the platform about to board a train. She is in a black skirt and gray top. Most of the other people on the platform are also young women in black. She asks a conductor if this is the right train.

BRIGITTE
Excuse me, sir. Excuse me.

CONDUCTOR
(surprised)
Oh, hello! Yes, ma'am, how can I help you?

BRIGITTE
Can you tell me if this is the train from Boston to New York?

CONDUCTOR
Oh, well, yes. All the trains are from Boston to New York, or going the other way around. Only way the rails go from here.

BRIGITTE
Oh, I see.

CONDUCTOR
Can't get to Hartford or to Worcester. Be nice to go to Albany but got to go through New York. Can't even get to the Cape by rail. Real shame, I'd say. Folks'd like that. But it's the only way the rails run.

BRIGITTE
So which way is New York?

CONDUCTOR
New York, this track, this side. Boston, that track there, boards on the other side. If you're going to New York, you're in just the right spot. Train will pull in shortly.

BRIGITTE
Thank you, sir.

CONDUCTOR

No trouble at all.

The Conductor wanders away, helping other passengers. The platform in Providence is not very busy and she stands by herself until the train pulls in. People get out but she has to open the door herself and nobody is there to help her with her bag so she hoists it up herself. She finds a seat.

The train pulls out and we see the train from the outside and the little station almost touching the Atlantic Ocean. From here, she heads west. She watches the town pass out of sight then deep woods and then down to the great metropolis.

INT. ON THE TRAIN TO CHICAGO - LATER

At Grand Central she finds the departures board for the Chicago Express line. She has a sleeper berth and another woman comes in to share it. She is in her late forties and has two large suitcases. They sit in silence while the train pulls out. The watch New York rolling by out the windows.

CLAIRE
Where you headed, far?

BRIGITTE
Chicago. You?

CLAIRE
Not that far. Only about halfway, going to Cleveland. I'm Claire Pierpont. And you?

BRIGITTE
Mrs. Brigitte Riley. Pleased to meet you. Say, Cleveland, that's on the lake, isn't it?

CLAIRE
That's right. I grew up right on Lake Erie.

BRIGITTE
Going back home?

CLAIRE
Yes. Sadly, yes, I am.

BRIGITTE
Do you live in New York?

CLAIRE
Not anymore.

BRIGITTE
Why, what's happened?

CLAIRE
It's this damned war.

BRIGITTE
What do you mean?

CLAIRE
Look around. The City is booming. Everything is go-go-go, for this goddamned war effort. I just can't stand it. Not anymore.

BRIGITTE
Why? What's wrong with the war effort?

CLAIRE
You're young, you wouldn't understand. I was married for twenty-two years. We outlasted the Depression but this damned war is too much. It will kill us all. It is madness on a global scale. I have get out, get away from this upside-down world.

BRIGITTE
Are you leaving... your husband?

CLAIRE
He was killed over there, six months ago. Career Army officer, been all over the world. Stationed in posts in the Himalayas, East Africa and Mexico. And you know how he died?

BRIGITTE
No.

CLAIRE
In a training accident when an artillery shell exploded next to him - because some new, greenhorn recruit couldn't read the instructions on disarming the gun. Killed three men on the base in England, not even

fighting the enemy.

BRIGITTE
Oh, I'm so sorry! That's terrible.

CLAIRE
So now, here I am, going home a lonely widow.

BRIGITTE
Is your family there?

CLAIRE
My father is still alive. I am going to care for him.

BRIGITTE
I see. Good to be helpful.

CLAIRE
I have been helpful for nearly thirty years. Helping everybody else, my mother, my husband, now my father. And I look back and wonder why I didn't help myself once and a while? But I know the answer, it was easier not to. Easier to take the Army pay. Easier to live near a base. Easier to not work. Easier, safer. Easier not to take a risk. So pathetic, I've become. I look at myself and think, I wouldn't marry me. Too lazy, too scared all the time.

BRIGITTE
You're being too hard on yourself.

CLAIRE
I think that's why he took posts around the world, you know, to spend his life away from me. Did he take women in Sri Lanka or Ethiopia? I don't know, but I wouldn't blame him if he did. Why would he want to be with a dried-up hag like me?

BRIGITTE
Goodness! Didn't you have any children?

CLAIRE
T*sk!* For a year we tried, then I think he just gave up on me. For the next twenty years, he'd come home for a few weeks, and we'd have a

tumble or two and then he was bored with me. He couldn't wait to get back to the big world, cut loose the ball and chain.

BRIGITTE
Hmm, I don't know. I guess I hope you find some, something that makes you happy.

CLAIRE
Yes, I guess. Listen, I've been up all night, packing. I'm going to fold my bed out and get some sleep. Do you mind?

BRIGITTE
Not at all. I'll be here.

Claire folds out the bed and is quickly asleep.

Brigitte watches the landscape roll by.

INT. ON THE TRAIN TO CHICAGO - HOURS LATER

BRIGITTE is asleep and Claire gets up and looks out the window. Before long BRIGITTE is awake again with the train going over a bump.

CLAIRE
We're getting close now. Are you awake?

BRIGITTE
Chicago?

CLAIRE
No, Cleveland. We're through Youngstown and will be downtown in a little while. Did you get some sleep?

BRIGITTE
Yes, I didn't know I was so run down.

CLAIRE
Listen, while I've still got a few minutes, I want to set something right. What I said.

BRIGITTE
What do you mean?

CLAIRE
What I said about my husband and our marriage, that's not right. I did love him. And I know he loved me, in his way. Part of his way was to get out of my way, let me grow and do what I wanted. That was very generous. And if I didn't do much with myself, well, that's not his fault.

BRIGITTE
I see.

CLAIRE
I just didn't want you to go away and think that he might have been a bad husband. He wasn't. He was a good man, a very decent man. And I loved him. And I miss him terribly. So, if you ever hear or read anything about Colonel Christopher Pierpont, know that he was a good soldier and a good husband.

51

BRIGITTE
OK.

CLAIRE
And I didn't ask you about your man. I'm sorry. Will you tell me about him?

BRIGITTE
Ohhhh. He was killed in France.
(sighs)

CLAIRE
I'm sorry. A widow so young. This damned war is ripping the country apart. Did you notice, at Grand Central, or on the platform, all of the young women - in black?

BRIGITTE
No. I only saw my own.

CLAIRE
Look. Because for every soldier killed, there is a widow or a mother wearing black, and so often travelling to see family to break the news and bring the grief. Up and down this train, every train. It is a season of widows.

BRIGITTE
Yes.

CLAIRE
But how many seasons will we have to endure, to carry on, holding on to the pain in my heart? I'm sorry. I'm so sorry.

BRIGITTE
He was nice. We were in love.

CLAIRE
How long were you married?

BRIGITTE
Forty-four days.

CLAIRE
(gasps!)

That's awful!

BRIGITTE
I don't think I know what it means yet. It was only six weeks ago I got the notice. I'm bringing it to his mother.

CLAIRE
Where, Chicago?

BRIGITTE
Montana. I don't even know how I'll get there. But Charley said, it's a big state and hard to miss when you get pointed at it. So I'm just pointing myself and going.

Train whistle sounds, brakes grinding and lurches to a stop.

Claire gets her bags down and puts them in the passageway.

CLAIRE
Listen, I've got to go but I want to share one thing with you. It's to make your life for yourself. Don't sacrifice yourself for somebody else's happiness. Or you will end up like me. Goodbye.

BRIGITTE
Goodbye Mrs. Pierpont. I hope you find happiness.

CLAIRE
You too, dear.

Claire exits the train.

Soon two young women, looking like sisters, in black, sit in BRIGITTE's cabin.

BRIGITTE
Hello. Are you going to Chicago?

KAREN
Uh-huh. South Side.

KATHY
Kinda west. Cicero. You know it?

BRIGITTE

No. Does the train stop there?

KATHY
No.

KAREN
The El.

BRIGITTE
The El?

KAREN
Elevated train. Gets you around town. Never been?

BRIGITTE
Chicago? No.

KATHY
Ah, you'll have a big time.

The train whistle sounds, doors slam and it lurches forward.

BRIGITTE
So, you're going home?

KAREN
Yeah.

KATHY
We were in Pittsburgh.

BRIGITTE
Oh.

KAREN
For a funeral.

BRIGITTE
Oh. Right. The black.

KAREN
You coming from a funeral?

BRIGITTE

Not yet, no. Who's was it?

KAREN
The funeral?

BRIGITTE
Yeah, in Pittsburgh.

KATHY
Our cousin, Jim's. He was killed, in It'ly.

BRIGITTE
My husband died in France.

KAREN
Yeah, tough times these days. Real rough.

BRIGITTE
So, you live in Chicago?

KAREN
Cicero, yeah.

BRIGITTE
Do you work? I mean, have jobs?

KATHY
Oh yeah! Of course. We live just down the street from a tubing plant.
Both work there.

BRIGITTE
Tubing?

KATHY
Yeah, you know, steel tubes, copper, brass, you name it.

BRIGITTE
I see.

KAREN
Listen, I'm bushed. I've got to get some shuteye if I'm going to make
it to the production line tomorrow. You mind if we pull out this bed?

BRIGITTE

No, go ahead. Both of you?

KATHY
It's a sister-act. Right?

KAREN
(laughs)
Sister act, yeah! That's it.

They pull out the bed on one side of the cabin. They both lie down together, fully dressed. They snuggle together and are soon both asleep.

BRIGITTE stares at them for a minute, wondering at how different they are.

Outside the land is flat with gray overcast sky. It is winter so the fields are ragged with harvested stalks of corn for miles and miles. Soon the monotony has BRIGITTE asleep as well.

INT. ON THE TRAIN TO CHICAGO - HOURS LATER, NIGHT

Karen gets up, and moving around, bumps BRIGITTE awake.

KAREN
Oh, sorry about that. Didn't mean to wake you.

BRIGITTE
It's OK. Where are we?

KAREN
Through Gary. I'm going to the club car for a cup of coffee. Want to come with?

BRIGITTE
Um, sure. OK.

Brigitte gets herself arranged and they go out, down the corridor to the lounge car. A porter takes their orders and they have cups of coffee as they sit in a booth.

KAREN
You said France, is that right?

BRIGITTE
Yes. Six weeks ago, in the invasion.

KAREN
That's too bad. I'm sorry.

BRIGITTE
It's done now.

KAREN
He was your husband?

BRIGITTE
Yes. For forty-four whole days.

KAREN
That's it?

BRIGITTE
We met, got married and a month later he shipped out. Forty-four lovely, beautiful days.

KAREN
Aww, you got robbed. That's a raw deal there. You have a picture of him?

BRIGITTE
Oh my god, no, I don't. I don't even have a picture of him. I can't believe it.

KAREN
Well, better luck next time. You're a pretty girl. You'll find a fella in town. That's no trouble. Like falling off a log.

BRIGITTE
But I just became a widow.

KAREN
Men don't much care, seems like.

BRIGITTE
I suppose you're right.

KAREN
Of course I'm right. Now Kathy, she thinks she's God's gift to men.

BRIGITTE
What do you mean?

KAREN
I mean, if the fella isn't willing to bend down and kiss her fat-ass whenever she says so, why, she gives him the heave-ho!

BRIGITTE
She can do that?

KAREN
You wouldn't believe what men will do for her.

BRIGITTE
Really?

KAREN
Why, there was this one guy, I can never remember his name, I just called him Slim. So, there was this guy, Slim, and she had him wrapped around her little finger. Take her out to fancy restaurants. Buy her gifts. Drive her all over town. It was ridiculous.

BRIGITTE
Why did he do that?

KAREN
The way she tells it Slim just wanted a woman to be nice to him, listen to him a little bit. And to not make fun of him for being kind of tall and...

BRIGITTE
Slim?

KAREN
Yeah! That's it. So she would listen to him gas on about whatever tomato-can-head idea he ever had, and he would do anything she wanted. I couldn't take it. He would think up the most silly, lame-brained ideas like he was some kind of genius, like Edison. He was one of those guys who never realized how dumb he really was. Sheesh! I tell ya.

BRIGITTE
(laughs)
Sounds like she got a kick out of it.

KAREN
We both got a kick out of it! She'd come home and tell me what-all he'd been talking about, and we'd laugh and laugh until we were about to split-open. The guy was a certified dip-stick.

BRIGITTE
(laughs)
You're funny. You work together?

KAREN
Yeah, at the Precision Products Tubing Plant, number Four. It's all a waste of time but the money's good. And good money is worth having. Make your own rules, do whatever you want.

BRIGITTE
That's right.

KAREN
At the funeral, my cousin's, all my other girl-cousins, they're married and they stay at home with kids. I'd be bored out of my mind. They barely get to say B*oo!* without the husband making a stink about whatever is on his mind, which usually ain't much. The usual, I bet. Anyway, I never wanted that, any of it. Keep those ding-bat kids to yourselves.

BRIGITTE
You don't want a husband? No children?

KAREN
Not my style. Never saw a swinging dick yet that made me want to hike my skirt. *Keep it in yer pants,* I tell em.

BRIGITTE
What about your parents?

KAREN
Mom lives down the street. We have a big soup on Sundays. Her sister lives next door to her on one side, and the other sister on the other side. My no-account uncle lives with her.

BRIGITTE
With your mother?

KAREN
My aunt, on the other side. My aunt, she married a guy who ran a nightclub, an entertainment place, a speakeasy. He got shot one afternoon taking a delivery, I guess it was from the wrong guys. Anyway, Aunt Bertha has been by herself ever since, so Uncle Tommy moved in with her. And like I said, every Sunday, it's soup and the same old stories about how Uncle Tommy had a line on something really great, but it never comes through. That guy's whole life is nothing but things falling through his fingers. Can't catch a break, I guess.

BRIGITTE
That's a tough way to go through life.

KAREN
That's what I said so I made my own luck. Got a job, got some money. We paid for the house so nobody can take it away.

BRIGITTE
But what if your sister gets married?

KAREN
Well, I don't worry too much about that.

BRIGITTE
Oh. None of my business but, why not?

KAREN
Let's say, she ain't the marrying type.

BRIGITTE
What do mean?

KAREN
Let's keep it at that. Listen, we'd better get back. We'll be at Union Station before you know it.

BRIGITTE
OK.

They get up and make their way back to the cabin.

Kathy is there and has everything folded up and packed, but her hair is unkempt.

KAREN
What happened to you? You look like you've been holding your head out the window.

KATHY
Yeah, I was wagging my tongue. No, I got up to take a leak.

KAREN
You fall in?

KATHY
It was just a bit more, substantial, is all.

KAREN
Great, now I don't have to hear you on the El, complaining about having to crap between the stations.

KATHY
Yeah, pretty nice, huh?

KAREN
You're a real queen, you know that?

KATHY
I'm glad you noticed, since my crown is in my valise.

KAREN
Your valise? I got your valise - right here.

The train whistles, grinds and yanks to a stop.

BRIGITTE
It has been a pleasure to meet you.

KAREN
You too. Take care of yourself.

BRIGITTE
Thanks. You too.

They all gather their things and empty out of the train into the grand station. The station is bustling with travelers going in all directions.

INT. TRAIN TO THE TWIN CITIES - MORNING

Inside Chicago Union Station, Brigitte finds the Departures board and sees the train for Minneapolis on another platform. She goes to the train, boards and looks out at the hustle and bustle in the station. She starts to notice so many women in black mourning clothes. As she watches it seems like there are more and more widows in the station until the only people going to and from trains are women in black, young and old. It is a whirling spectacle of grief and death. She turns away and is soon asleep.

When the train jerks into motion, nearly an hour later, she jolts up and is awake. She is by herself in the cabin.

A conductor comes by and punches her ticket. It's late at night so she pulls the bed out and goes to sleep.

Hours later, the sun is coming up and the train is crossing the Mississippi River. She wakes up and sees the sun reflecting on the water. There is ice at the edges of the river.

Brigitte takes out a sheet of railroad stationery and begins to write.

BRIGITTE
(writing)
Dear Mrs. Riley, I am writing to you from the train, so I apologize for the wobbly handwriting. I will arrive in Minneapolis today and I will post this letter there. Then I will find a train heading toward Montana. I might stay the night in a hotel, just to get out of these train cars for a night.

I should be able to arrive in Medicine Lake by the end of the week, but I don't know for sure.

Mrs. Riley, I'm writing because I promised Charley that I would visit you if he was gone for too long. As you know, he was shipped out for the battle in Europe. I hope he is safe and being a good sailor.

Anyway, I don't know what to expect in Medicine Lake but I will be there in a few days. I look forward to meeting you.

Mrs. Charles Riley.

She puts the letter in an envelope and addresses it.

She takes out another sheet of paper and begins.

BRIGITTE
(writing)
Dear Mother,

I am writing this from the train to Minnesota. I have already been through New York, Cleveland and Chicago. This morning I just crossed over the Mississippi river.

A woman riding from New York said, it is a season of widows, because all of the men being killed in the war. I see it now, with so many women in black, on the platforms. And I see myself there too, a woman in mourning, moving around the country alone.

I know you think I am just a schoolgirl, but I have been married and now I am a widow. And I am crossing the country, by myself, to visit Charley's mother.

The distance from Rhode Island has me thinking about the sweet pleasures at home, by the sea, but the big blue sky out here gives me hope for the future. I am sorry I did not join you for the summer social season in Providence. I'm sorry that I left you on harsh terms. I am sorry that I didn't invite you to my wedding and I am sorry that you never got to meet Charley. I know you won't forgive me, but I'm sorry anyway.

Take good care of yourself and I'll be back East before too long. Love, your daughter, B.

She folds up the letter into an envelope and addresses it. She licks the back to seal it shut.

EXT. PLATFORM AT CULBERTSON, MONTANA - LATE MORNING - TWO DAYS LATER

63

The platform is in Culbertson is little more than and asphalt strip beside the tracks. There is a low brick station building but it is just a ticket booth and a porter's closet.

The day is bright but cold. Sun is up but thin, wispy clouds float lazily in the sky. The overnight frost has melted.

The station is not usually manned full-time, but the train company called from Minneapolis Station to say that there would be an arrival at Culbertson today. One person, plus mail.

Railroad Stationmaster Harold Jepson walked across the small-town street, in his Railroad vest and trousers. He lives across from the station with his wife, Ingrid. They are both in their late fifties. Harold is a heavy-set man with a prodigious mustache, combed out, waxed and turned up at the edges. He stands on the platform, looking at his pocket watch and then down the tracks over the endless horizon. He hears the train before he sees it, so he gets a hand cart and waits in the shade for the mechanical beast to arrive.

Suddenly the train is at the station and pulls up to a stop. With a great burst of steam, the huge machine ticks quietly.

The Engineer comes down and they make arrangements for the train to take on water. There is general coming and going of engineers and porters, with huge noises of whooshing water going into the steam train. Near the back of the train a door slides open on the Postal car and tosses down a sack of mail.

A porter emerges from one of the carriages and puts down a small footstool. Brigitte appears at the door and steps down onto the platform, such as it is. A porter inside hands down her bags. She tips the porter a coin.

BRIGITTE
Thank you.

HAROLD
(approaches)
Hallo! Hallo. You must be our arrival.

BRIGITTE
Yes, I guess I am.

HAROLD
Please, step this way. The train will be leaving soon, and it can be very dangerous.

Harold hustles Brigitte away from the train, along with her bags. He signs off with the engineer and the might train blows a great whistle-blast. It jerks the wheels into motion and before long it is gone over the horizon.

BRIGITTE
Is this Culbertson?

HAROLD
Montana, yes ma'am.

BRIGITTE
Is there a place to take a bus?

HAROLD
A bus?

BRIGITTE
I am trying to get to Medicine Lake. Do you know where that is?

HAROLD
Know where it is, why my brother Magnus and I grew up there. He's still farming, all through the Dustbowl. I got out when I could.

BRIGITTE
I see.

HAROLD
(seeing her clearly)
Well, if you are heading to Medicine Lake, we'll have to find you a ride.

BRIGITTE
I'd like to get something to eat, if you don't mind. A café or someplace to get a bowl of soup. Is that possible?

HAROLD
I'm kind of the official greeter around here and I can tell you there is not much. I'll tell you what, follow me and I'll have Ingrid fix you up

something. I am headed home for lunch anyhow.

BRIGITTE
Is it far?

HAROLD
Just across the street, miss. You look like you've come some way to get here. Ingrid will be interested to hear of your travels.

BRIGITTE
Are you sure? I am happy to pay.

HAROLD
No need for that. Just follow me.

Harold takes her bags and they go back across the street to his house. It is a concrete block building with a big window on the street and a second level where the bedrooms are. It is a modest but nice house in a modest but nice town.

INT. JEPSON HOUSE - SAME TIME

Brigitte is introduced and Ingrid looks her over and hands her a cup of coffee.

INGRID
Sit, girl, sit. Rest. It looks like you have sailed across the seas. Where are you from?

BRIGITTE
Back East. Rhode Island.

INGRID
That's the really small one right, the really small state?

BRIGITTE
Yes, that's it. By the Atlantic Ocean.

INGRID
Why that must be something, the ocean. We've never been that far. Harold took his train to Missoula for a postal training class.

BRIGITTE
A postal class?

INGRID
Harold is the postman in town, but we do it together. Sometimes in the bad weather we have to go together to get the mail out. Most folks get mail here at the station, but there are some special deliveries you know, like telegrams.

BRIGITTE
I see.

INGRID
Been a lot of telegrams lately. About the men over there, fighting the war. Lost two Roosevelt County boys just last week, the news came through. The shame of it.

BRIGITTE
Yes. It's really sad.

Ingrid makes some sandwiches and heats up some soup. Harold returns and they all sit down at the table for lunch.

HAROLD
Did she tell you, she's heading to Medicine Lake?

BRIGITTE
Yes, that's right.

INGRID
Are you going to take her?

BRIGITTE
Oh really, that's not necessary.

INGRID
Yes, it is. There really isn't another way to get there.

BRIGITTE
Oh!

INGRID
Listen, after you have a bite to eat, lie down on the davenport for a little while. Then Harold can take you up there.

HAROLD
Not today, I'm afraid. There is mail to sort. Got quite a parcel today.

INGRID
Then I will take her. I'll take the car.
(to Brigitte)
It's a Marmon!

HAROLD
"Mechanical Masterpiece", that's what they say. Sixteen cylinders!

BRIGITTE
Is that good?

HAROLD
Oh, it pulls like a locomotive! And, now you mention it, maybe a drive up to Medicine would be just the thing.

INGRID
I wouldn't hear of it, dear, what with all that mail. I insist. I'll drive her.
(to Brigitte)
Who are you going to see in Medicine Lake?

BRIGITTE
Mrs. Riley.

INGRID
(surprised!)
Liesl Bachmann? Well, why didn't you say so. My stars, it's high time I had a sit down with her.

HAROLD
You know her?

INGRID
Why there's Bachmann's all around. She was one of, what was it, eleven, twelve? Kith-and-kin from Butte to Saskatoon. Years ago, you know, I was on the basketball team with her sister Gretta. They called us the Speedy Sisters - because we ran around, too fast for our own good. Oh, the times we had!

HAROLD

It was high time I made a married woman of ye', past time really. But that's all settled issue now.

INGRID
Ach! I'll give Liesl a call right now.

Ingrid gets up and dials the phone, talking to the operator, then connects with Liesl.

INGRID
(into phone - in German)
Hallo Liesl. Es ist Ingrid Jepson aus Culbertson. Ja. Hören Sie, hier ist eine Frau, come to see you. Brigitte aus Rhode Island. Can we visit you today? Ja. Jawohl. OK. Wir sind später da. See you then.
(hangs up)
Ja, she'll be waiting for us.

BRIGITTE
This is so unexpected. I really can't thank you enough.

INGRID
So, you go have a lie-down over there. You'll feel better and then we'll take a drive later.

Brigitte does as she is told and is soon asleep in the front room.

HAROLD
I could have taken her.

INGRID
As Post Mistress, I will stamp her as a Special Delivery Parcel.

HAROLD
(chuckles)
Well, in that case...

INGRID
Case closed.

I/E. DRIVE TO MEDICINE LAKE - AFTERNOON

Ingrid drives the big Marmon. It has sixteen cylinders and a very long hood. The Montana winters have dulled the famous "Jewel Colors" paintwork, and it is twenty years-old now, but it is still an impressive luxury automobile. One of the few true rivals for Roll-Royce in America, the car rides like a dream.

They cruise along across the rolling prairie with few trees and endless horizons. Both desolate and exhilarating, the Big Sky has Brigitte in awe of the countryside.

INGRID
Can you drive a car?

BRIGITTE
Not one this big! Never!

INGRID
Oh, it's not so bad. No traffic, straight road, beautiful day. Nice day for a drive.

BRIGITTE
When did you learn to drive?

INGRID
Growing up on a farm, you have to learn to drive everything, horses, teams, cars, tractors. The only way.

BRIGITTE
Did you always want to live out here?

INGRID
Out here? This is home. My family is all around. My life has memories at every crossroads. I am not 'out here', I'm home.

BRIGITTE
I mean, like farming and with animals. You know.

INGRID
Well, I met Harold, and he didn't want to be a farmer. He wanted to be on the railroad. And I thought, well I wouldn't mind at all if I

didn't have to steal eggs from the chickens or get up early to milk any Holsteins. And then when the Postmaster position became open, well, that was it. He was a prize catch then, I tell you! My mother was so proud, a Post Master!

BRIGITTE
Why is a Post Master so good?

INGRID
Dear girl, look around. Do you see lots and lots of good jobs? Hmmm? No, sodbusting and chasing beef cattle. But, you know what happens when you are the Postman?

BRIGITTE
What?

INGRID
You get a check, from the US government! Every month! And it doesn't bounce and it is real dollars. Not company scrip. You know how they pay coal miners in the winter? With coal. Not money, coal. But not for the Postman. And Post Master, of the entire station! And he is Station Master for the railroad. They pay too!

BRIGITTE
I see. That is good.

INGRID
During the Depression, you know who was the most trusted and reliable man in town?

BRIGITTE
Harold?

INGRID
Harold. Because everyone knew that we made real money, and were not in the pocket of the banker or the head of the mine, Tim Riley.

BRIGITTE
Wait, Tim Riley? What about him?

INGRID

He married Liesl when he got back from the mining school and started at the Bentz mine. When he became the big boss, well, it was just when the market crashed, and the crops couldn't get harvested because it cost more than leaving them. And there was no money, but they kept digging at the mine. And he paid them in company scrip, to buy things at the company store. But there was no way to get ahead, and you saw families crushed by the company. When the first man dove into the pit, out of despair, then another, and then another. Families just left, abandoned their houses, their land. Just drove away. But Riley kept the machines grinding out there.

BRIGITTE
What about Liesl? What about Charley?

INGRID
Did she turn a blind eye? Did she not know? How could she not? All around, everything was falling down.

BRIGITTE
But what about Charley?

INGRID
He was a good boy, a sweet boy, like his mother. She was a Pacifist in the Great War, not that they would send her, but she was against it altogether. I saw Charley play baseball once, on the Fourth of July. Just there, you see?

They slow as they come to the edge of town and a manicured baseball field sits as the crown jewel of the town park.

BRIGITTE
Oh, I see. Yes.

INGRID
She lives up here, on First Avenue.

She wheels the car through town and stops in a short driveway, in front of a sturdy brick house.

Liesl Riley comes out of the front door. She is a small woman in her late fifties with flowing grey hair, pulled back.

LIESL

Ingrid! So wonderful to see you!

INGRID
Oh, Liesl. I am so glad to see you well.

LIESL
Yes, thank you. And this is?

INGRID
Her name is Brigitte and she comes from Rhode Island.

LIESL
Ah, yes, I got your letter, just this morning. You are the new Missus Riley. Won't you come in?

They all go inside to a sitting room where a set of coffee cups, a percolator and ashtrays are on the table.

MOTHER'S GRIEF

INT. LIESL RILEY'S HOUSE - LATE AFTERNOON

The house is spacious, sturdy and well appointed. This was the house of the general manager of the Bentz mine nearby and an important house for the neighborhood. The furniture is fashionable for the 1930's and not much has changed since Timothy Riley, her husband has died four years ago.

Brigitte, Ingrid and Liesl sit and pour coffee. Liesl lights a cigarette, offers one to Ingrid and they take time to enjoy the smoke.

BRIGITTE
This house is lovely. How long have you lived here?

LIESL
It was built in 1914 by the previous manager at the mine. When Tim took over, we got the house. That was in thirty-five so, a while.

INGRID
Did you buy it then?

LIESL
Yes, the company owned it but Tim bought it from them, on their loan scheme. Very attractive terms. Now it is just me though.

INGRID
How is Gretta, by the way? I haven't seen her for years.

LIESL
I saw her at Christmastime last year, in Bismarck. She has two sons in the Army and two daughters and some grandchildren. She is doing very well. Thank you. And how are you and Harold doing?

INGRID
Oh, very well. Harold is keeping busy. He had a pain in his chest this spring so we went down to the doctor. But he's alright.

LIESL
What did the doctor say?

INGRID
You won't believe it, but he said that it was probably from
indigestion, from my potato dumplings. The quack!

LIESL
That was it? Tummy trouble?

INGRID
(takes a long draw)
Well, while Harold was getting dressed, the doctor also had the nerve
to tell me that if I would,
(blows out smoke)
Jerk his Jepson twice-a-week, he would live to be one hundred.

LIESL
(Hoots!)
Ohhh! What did you say?

INGRID
I said, that's too much! And he said, ok, once a week, but he will
drop-dead when he's eighty.

LIESL
(laughs)
Oh, ha! HA! Oh, you are naughty, Ingrid. Naughty girl.

INGRID
(laughs and sips coffee)
Well, you know, duties-of-the-wife.

LIESL
(chuckling)
Oh, too well, too well. And you Bri-Git-te, a new wife, listening to
these old hens. I'm sorry that I was not there for the wedding. Was it
lovely?

BRIGITTE
It was a beautiful day. I wore a yellow dress, with a hat. Charley wore
his dress uniform. And we went down to City Hall, and waited with
the other brides and grooms until it was our turn. Then, sign-on-the-
dotted-line, and out we went. That was it.

LIESL

And when Charley was shipped out, what did you do?

BRIGITTE
Oh, I don't know. I was so sad. He was gone and I was alone. I think I just sat and stared out the window for a week.

LIESL
Hmmm.

BRIGITTE
And then, one day it rained and I thought I'd better get moving. So I packed up things in our apartment and went looking for a job in town. I started the next day in the office of the Newport WaterWorks.

LIESL
The WaterWorks? For the town water system?

BRIGITTE
Yes, you know, billing, connections, service changes. That sort of thing. Not an important job but they needed the help and I liked working.

LIESL
But why did you come here then?

BRIGITTE
Because I got a letter from the government.

LIESL
Oh no...

BRIGITTE
They said that Charley was killed, in France.

INGRID
(gasps!)
Oh my! Oh no.

LIESL
So it's true then. My Charley really is gone.

INGRID
What do you mean, Liesl?

LIESL
I have this dream, over and over, that a woman comes to the house
and hands me the telegram, and it says that Charley is dead.

*Brigitte fishes around in her handbag and pulls out an envelope with
official stamps outside.*

BRIGITTE
This letter.

She hands it to Liesl but Liesl puts it on the table, unopened.

INGRID
Aren't you going to read it?

LIESL
I already know what it says. And, what difference does it make? If he
is dead then the details don't matter. He's not coming back. That's it.

When my husband died, it was a sudden thing. He was working,
going to the mine. He came home and I made him dinner. He said he
wanted to go to bed so I kissed him, and he went upstairs. Later,
when I went up to be with him in bed, he was already cold. He just
didn't wake up. And I cried and I howled and I cursed God for being
so cruel to me. And when we buried him, do you remember?

INGRID
Oh, Liesl, I'm so sorry. I'm so sorry. Yes, I was there. It was so cold
that day. I don't think I can remember a colder day for a burial.

LIESL
I knew he was gone, his spirit, his life, but his body was still there.
And then the thing that hurt the most was to lower him into that
frozen grave. I stood there but I wanted to jump in.

INGRID
Oh dear.

LIESL
But I had Charley, you know. I wasn't alone. Not yet. And Charley, I
wanted him to come back, to be a journalist, if that's what he wanted.

Sure, write about Sheridan County, the crop prices, the wheat yield, the parade on the Fourth of July, all of it. But to come back. To come back. But he's not, he's never, he's, he's... never coming back. Not now. Not ever. And I am both a widow and a childless mother. Oh, black day.

Ingrid goes to Liesl and puts her arms around her.

Brigitte sits on Liesl's other side and puts her arms around Liesl. They all hug. Liesl cries and they hold her.

LIESL
(quietly)
Ok. Ok. I'm Ok. Thank you. Thank you both.

Brigitte and Ingrid go back to sitting separately. Liesl pours coffee for Ingrid and Brigitte.

BRIGITTE
I am so sorry, Mrs. Riley.

LIESL
Thank you - Missus Riley. I'm sorry for you as well.

INGRID
So sad, my dear. But can I tell you, do you know what else the doctor said?

LIESL
(confused)
No, what else did the doctor say?

INGRID
I said, well, what about me? How do I live to be one-hundred?

BRIGITTE
What did he say?

INGRID
He said that the women who live to one-hundred all have the same thing in common, a community of other women who care for each other. The Convent Paradox, they call it. And he said that the real cause of death for women is loneliness. And, Liesl, I don't want you

to be lonely. I want you to come back with me to Culbertson. Stay with us for a while, won't you?

LIESL
But what about Brigitte here?

BRIGITTE
I could stay with you.

INGRID
What about your job, with the water works?

BRIGITTE
They've already replaced me. And maybe I could work for the water works here? I could stay with you for a while and work.

LIESL
I would like that very much. I have plenty of room here and the company would do me good.

BRIGITTE
Well then, there we go.

INGRID
But how long will you stay?

BRIGITTE
I don't know. I've never been to these parts. Maybe I'll have a look around and see how it goes.

INGRID
Be careful or you'll get planted in and the years will fly by.

BRIGITTE
Is that the worst thing? I don't want to go back to Newport, I'll tell you that much.

Liesl picks up the letter and reads it.

LIESL
(reading)
"24 June 1944: Mrs. Charles Riley:

The Admiral of the Navy for the European Theater has entrusted me to express his deep regret that your husband, Charles Bachmann Riley, Sailor, was killed in action as part of Operation Neptune at Omaha Beach in Normandy, France on 12 June 1944. His deployment, battleship USS Nevada (BB-39) was attacked by enemy aircraft and he was killed in the attack. Sailor Riley was reported to be well liked and brave in his duties for the United States Navy. The Admiral extends his deepest sympathy to you and your family in your loss. - Capt. JS Simmons (BB-39)"

BRIGITTE
I've read it a hundred times, over and over.

LIESL
Well-liked and brave.

BRIGITTE
That was him.

LIESL
That was him.

INGRID
I'm sorry Liesl. Please let me know if there is anything I can do.

LIESL
Thank you. You are a kind comfort, Ingrid. So good to see an old friend. And thank you for bringing Brigitte here.

Ingrid gets up so they all get up.

INGRID
Yes, I should be getting back, before the dark comes down.

LIESL
Yes, for Harold. You don't want to keep his Mister- Jepson waiting.

INGRID
(chuckles)
Oh, no. Eighty is long enough for him. Ha!

LIESL

Ha! Goodbye, Ingrid Norberg.

INGRID
Goodbye, Liesl Bachmann.

Ingrid goes out and Liesl and Brigitte watch the fancy car drive away.

LIESL
You can put your things upstairs. Take the room on the right.

Brigitte ascends the stairs with her luggage.

I/E VARIOUS LOCATIONS, VARIOUS TIMES

Scene of Liesl and Brigitte walking through town together.

Scene of Brigitte talking to a woman about a job with the County Office in town.

A scene of Liesl and Brigitte watching a movie at the town cinema together.

Seasons pass and we see Liesl and Brigitte working in the garden together, planting and then harvesting vegetables and fruits.

Scene of Brigitte working at a desk in the County Office, on the phone, with clients.

Eight years pass.

Scene of Liesl, ill in bed at night.

INT. LISEL'S BEDROOM - NIGHT

Liesl has been ill for nearly a year and the end is near.

LIESL
Some water please, dear?

BRIGITTE

Yes, mother.

She hands Liesl a stubby coffee cup with water.

LIESL
Brigitte, thank you. You are such a great help to me. I don't know what would have become of me without you. I don't think I ever thanked you enough for staying with me.

BRIGITTE
Of course, yes. It's nice.

LIESL
But I will gone soon. You've wasted enough of your life on me. I want you to move on. Find a companion. Marry a good man.

BRIGITTE
I'll never forget Charley. You know that. And I haven't wasted my life. At school we used to debate if a woman should marry for love or for money, but the real question was how to decide for yourself what is right. And I am glad to spend this time with you. I have no regrets.

LIESL
He's been gone for eight years now. You have to let him go. Let yourself be happy. Do that for me, will you?

BRIGITTE
Yes, mother. Now try to sleep. We'll go into town tomorrow.

LIESL
Yes, alright. Thank you dear.

BRIGITTE
Good night, mother.

Brigitte goes out and turns out the light.

EXT. CEMETERY - FIVE DAYS LATER - MORNING

A small group is gathered in the spring sunshine. Harold Jepson is there but Ingrid is not. Wayne and Reuben Webster are there. A priest and some people from the church, as well as some distant Bachmann relations.

Brigitte watches as the priest says the prayers and the casket is lowered into the grave. When the service is over, people begin to disperse.

HAROLD
Mrs. Riley, I'm sorry for the day. She was a heck of a woman.

BRIGITTE
Thank you, Mr. Jepson. And I heard that you lost Ingrid last year. I'm sorry for you.

HAROLD
Thank you, dear girl. I'm lost without her. What is a man supposed to do alone?

BRIGITTE
Just keep an eye on the trains, I guess.

HAROLD
Yep. OK.

Harold goes and it is only Brigitte by the grave.

BRIGITTE
Good by Missus Riley. Say hello to Charley for me.

She gets in her own car and drives back to town.

END

THE DAUGHTER PROBLEM

RICK REGAN

2020

INT - FARMHOUSE FRONT ROOM - FRIDAY EVENING
In the main living room of WAYNE WEBSTER and his brother
REUBEN WEBSTER. The house is outside of Medicine Lake, Montana,
near the North Dakota and Canadian borders, near the edge of the Fort
Peck Indian Reservation. Flat in every direction and very few people.
The year is 1956, in the fall. The few trees in the yard have all lost their
leaves already.

WAYNE and REUBEN are playing cribbage, an old-time card game
with a small board and pegs in holes.

WAYNE
Ah, Roy G Biv! Cripes.

Wayne moves his pegs forward but not very far.

REUBEN
Ya, they roll like that.

WAYNE
Lyle comin' by?

REUBEN
He took another shift at the shaft, overtime. He'll be around
tomorrow.

WAYNE
Deal 'em.

REUBEN
(flips a card)
Go.

They both lay down cards and count up the points.

*W*AYNE
Ah, no luck tonight. You've got it.

REUBEN
Beer and a bump?

WAYNE
Sure, yeah.

Reuben shuffles the cards and resets the board, while Wayne assembles some cocktail glasses, a bowl with ice, an unlabeled rye whiskey bottle and some cans of Blatz beer. He brings a tray to the table and they take turns preparing drinks. They both have poured single shots of liquor.

REUBEN
You can't drink all day...

WAYNE
If you don't start in the morning.

BOTH
Cheers!

They down the shots and double-tap the glass on the table. They open the beers and sip those.

REUBEN
Did I tell ya' I was out up to Plentywood this week?

WAYNE
Oh, did ya?

REUBEN
Ya.

WAYNE
Groceries?

REUBEN
Yup.

WAYNE
Hmm. Long way.

REUBEN
Ya, but I stopped by Hurst's as well.

WAYNE
Just to see what's new?

REUBEN
No, I took my Browning 30-30 in. The trigger needs adjustment and I
don't trust myself with it.

WAYNE
Yup, it's a job for a professional when you're dealing with triggers.
Too loose for ya?

REUBEN
It would stick real hard. Instead of a smooth pull, ya know.

WAYNE
That would make you miss every time. What'd Hurst say?

REUBEN
He'd take a look and call me. Haven't heard from him though.

WAYNE
Funny, I was up that way myself this week.

REUBEN
Got a sticky trigger too?

WAYNE
No, I went up, then out Five. Out to the bend where Keme bought it.

REUBEN
Oh, that was sad.

WAYNE
Not a damned thing out there.

REUBEN
What got you thinking about it?

WAYNE
Well, Josephine, she's got a birthday coming up.

REUBEN
How old would she be?

WAYNE
She'll be eighteen, end of next week.

REUBEN
So it put you in mind of Keme?

WAYNE
That, and I ran into Joe Grey Hawk down at the grain co-op.

REUBEN
I haven't seen him in years. Is he back?

WAYNE
Just hauling a load, I guess.

REUBEN
You talk to him?

WAYNE
I said, "Hey, Joe, how come you're still driving?" I said that, I did.

REUBEN
What'd he say?

WAYNE
He said he moved across the line into Dakota, got a new license there. They just gave him one, I guess. Never looked into him, saw what he done.

REUBEN
I still remember that night. Coming up on ten year, isn't it?

WAYNE
It is.

REUBEN
How old was Josie then?

WAYNE
She was only eight years old when Joe Grey Hawk swerved his truck right into Keme. He said he never even knew he'd done it. Said he was reaching down the seat for something.

REUBEN
Whiskey bottle, most like.

They both refill the shot glasses, down the liquor and double-tap the table.

WAYNE
Poor Keme went into that ditch, blacked out. And then froze right there in his own car. Damned cold that night.

REUBEN
Colder than a well-digger's butt, for sure. But you went back to see it?

WAYNE
Like you said, it's coming up on ten years.

REUBEN
Ya.

WAYNE
I pulled off and walked the ground. It was an icy road that night. In clear day, why you could have rolled a bowling ball straight for ten miles until you got to that curve. Why them two was there at that time, just like that, out in the middle of nowheres? I don't know.

REUBEN
Where was he going, Keme?

WAYNE
He was up on the rez, to see his people.

REUBEN
Was he full Blackfoot?

WAYNE
Yeah, Assini. He was coming back home after a sweat lodge, his mother told me. Back to Colleen and Josephine.

REUBEN
And Joe Grey Hawk? He just got away with it?

WAYNE
You remember, don't ya? The paper in town had all the news about Keme Marten, and Colleen and Josie, with no info about what happened. And Joe come forward and said it must have been him, on account of him saying he was on that road, about that time. He said

he never knew he hit him or nothing.

REUBEN
He was just back from the war, wasn't he?

WAYNE
Right, he was. Someplace in Italy, he said. Well, the cops didn't have any real proof, and Joe, he come forward and all, and him being a war hero and all, so...

REUBEN
They let him go.

WAYNE
They let him go.

REUBEN
I remember going to their wedding, Keme and Colleen. That was a nice spring day, beautiful bride. So much hope.

WAYNE
(chokes up)
Beautiful bride. Her and Irene.

Wayne sips his beer and Reuben pours more whiskey. They drink and double-tap.

REUBEN
Ah, you suppose it had to happen that way, them being twins?

WAYNE
One without the other, you mean?

REUBEN
Right, like, they looked alike, talked alike, thought alike.

WAYNE
I suppose something must have been different between them because me and Keme are, were, about as different as two fellas could be.

REUBEN
Ach! You were like brothers, yourselves. Good looking gents, or used to be, strong, with a good heart. And both of ya, not-too-smart,

put together.

WAYNE
Ha!

REUBEN
Heh!

WAYNE
They were as beautiful a pair of queens as you'd ever see. Their smiles were like pure sunlight. Why Irene and Mother would battle like hens, and love every moment.

REUBEN
That was a dark day when they both went.

WAYNE
The darkest day.

REUBEN
And little Josie, how old was she then?

WAYNE
Eight when she lost her father. Twelve when she lost her mother.

REUBEN
And now coming up on eighteen. You've done right by her, Wayne. You really have.

WAYNE
Did I have a choice? I was the last one standing. Imagine if I'd have been killed in a bailing machine. What would have happened to them?

REUBEN
I suppose they'd have come to me.

WAYNE
Jiminy, they got lucky I'm still around. Three women, under your roof? That would have put the starch in your shirt.

REUBEN
I don't even want to think about losing you too, brother.

WAYNE
I don't suppose the walls of your kitchen have seen a woman inside there since Mother's been gone.

REUBEN
Ach! You know it's slim pickings out here.

WAYNE
Why, I saw the widow Riley just the other day, coming out of the *Honk'r Stop.* She'd be a frisky-fit for ya.

REUBEN
(derisive)
The widow Riley? No need to buy what is for rent.

WAYNE
She would be a woman with a robust appetite, for sure, but sore-lonely too, I think. *For rent,* that's unkind. And you sleeping in the cold bed every night.

REUBEN
Ah Wayne, a woman would want to civilize me. I've been too long on my own, too long alone.

WAYNE
Alone? You come here every night!

REUBEN
Oh, is that bad?

WAYNE
Of course, you are always welcome. Don't get jerked out of joint. That's not what I mean.

REUBEN
Well then?

WAYNE
It's just that you've got a lot of love in your heart and it seems a damned shame to deny the widow Riley what she wants most.

REUBEN
What's that?

WAYNE
Your money!

REUBEN
Ha!

WAYNE
Heh-heh! No, she's a nice girl. I invited her to Josie's party next week.

REUBEN
Have you?

WAYNE
Ah, it come out of my mouth before I was thinking. But I thought of you and her and it seemed the right thing. Just take a bath, would you?

REUBEN
Sure, and a new tie.

Reuben moves to pour more liquor. Wayne waves him off.

*WA*YNE
No more for me. Maeve will be around in a few minutes.

REUBEN
Ah, right.

WAYNE
Should keep my head clear.

REUBEN
And how is she, Maeve?

WAYNE
Fifteen going on fifty.

REUBEN
Fifty?

WAYNE
She says she wants to be a *farm-wife,* with a herd of kids and some buffalo cowboy. You'd think she was a sod-buster Pioneer, from the old days.

REUBEN
Where'd she get that idea?

WAYNE
Mystery to me. But with Marie in town, working at the bank, and
Josephine turning eighteen and going who-knows-where, Maeve
looks like she's putting down roots, under my feet.

REUBEN
How do you feel about that?

WAYNE
Ah, I think she should see some of the world, before she plants
herself up to her ears in Sher-i-dan County.

REUBEN
She's fifteen, but does she have a fella? Her own buffalo cowboy?

WAYNE
Not that she's told me, but she wouldn't anyway. This is when I wish
her mother was here. Speaking of being lonely.

REUBEN
I never understood that, Wayne. The two of them, *good skaters!,* to
fall into the ice. Twins, die together, the same way. Drown in the
frozen lake. Doesn't make any sense.

WAYNE
It was both or none with them. Twins, for sure. Could hardly separate
them.

REUBEN
And poor Josie, having to slot in between your two girls. Best as
could be done, I guess.

WAYNE
I guess. We done our best, I suppose.

REUBEN
Ya, I suppose. So, what about the party? What are you planning?

WAYNE
Me? Planning? Oh no! That's way over my head, or so they tell me.

The girls just say, "Please, pa, just stay out the way." So I go out haying. Always work to be done.

REUBEN
Heh! That Josie, she's real comical.

WAYNE
She's a strange girl. I love her to death but I don't understand half of what she's saying. I realize now that Marie, when she was still here, was translating for me, telling me what Josie was up to. I miss her a lot too.

REUBEN
How long has she been gone now?

WAYNE
A good year, I suppose.

REUBEN
She told me she was saving up to move to Toronto, get a job in a bank there. I told her I'd pony up five hundred dollars for the project, when the time come.

WAYNE
Did you?

REUBEN
Ya.

WAYNE
Well, you might better start counting out those bills.

REUBEN
Why's that?

WAYNE
The widow Riley asked me about my Marie. She said that she'd seen her in the bank. They talked. She said Marie hinted that she had a boyfriend and was eyeing making a big move.

REUBEN
Well, that's news. I'll ask her about it next week.

WAYNE
So will I. The name Ben Hair come up.

REUBEN
Ben Hair? What's she doing with him? Mother said that bunch isn't smart enough to play cards.

WAYNE
It's out of my hands. She's a grown woman.

REUBEN
But you're still her father.

WAYNE
I'm her father but it feels like the curse is closing in. You know what I mean? First Keme, then Irene and Colleen. Feels like it's coming for me now.

REUBEN
Ah, that's the whiskey talking. You're alright.

WAYNE
I don't know.

REUBEN
You make this?
(indicates the whiskey)

WAYNE
No, one of the Parnell boys, Irene's brother, Pat.

REUBEN
Tasty. They make it or just bring it across the border?

WAYNE
Just bring it over, I think. The Parnell's were never real whiskey makers. Not like Pa.

REUBEN
Still, it's nice stuff. Thanks.

WAYNE
Right.

REUBEN
I'll be on my way then. Leave you to it.

WAYNE
More hands make fast work.

REUBEN
Done working for today. See you tomorrow.

WAYNE
Good night, Roob.

REUBEN
G'night, Wayne.
(exits)

INT. - FARMHOUSE FRONT ROOM - LATER

Wayne is asleep in an overstuffed recliner. JOSEPHINE and MAEVE come in, see WAYNE asleep and tiptoe by him. He wakes up.

WAYNE
Hey, now. Hmm. Hey. What's, uh... How are you?

JOSEPHINE
Fine, Dad. You alright?

WAYNE
Sure, just checking the inside of my eyelids for cracks.

MAEVE
You were snoring, Dad.

WAYNE
Oh, well, that's to fool ya, into thinking I was asleep the whole time. But you won't catch me sleeping on the job. Did you eat?

MAEVE
It's Friday night, Dad.

WAYNE
Meaning?

JOSEPHINE

We had fish at the church.

WAYNE
Did you see anybody?

JOSEPHINE
Marie dropped in. She was with Ben Hair. Can you believe that?

WAYNE
Not so much. What do you think of the fella?

MAEVE
He's cute but he's not real smart. I don't know why she keeps him around.

WAYNE
Right. Me neither. Say, you have what you need for the party?

JOSEPHINE
Well, I think so. The circus tent goes up on Wednesday and the Hot Air Balloon comes on Thursday, but the clowns and the circus animals don't actually get here until Friday.

WAYNE
Circus tent?! Clowns? Hot air?

JOSEPHINE
I'm just kidding, Dad. It will just be some streamers and balloons. Simple and fun.

WAYNE
Ok. Well, if you need something, you know.

JOSEPHINE
OK, Dad.

WAYNE
I'm going to go hit the sack. Long day. You ladies staying up?

JOSEPHINE
For a little while.

WAYNE
OK. Sleep tight.

MAEVE
You too, Pop.

WAYNE exits upstairs to his bedroom.

JOSEPHINE fishes around in the cabinet and pulls out the whiskey bottle. She brings two glasses. MAEVE and JOSEPHINE sit at the table with small glasses of whiskey.

JOSEPHINE
(sniffs)
Whoo! Smooth.

MAEVE
(sniffs)
Woohuhoo! That's strong.

They clink glasses and sip, making faces at the strong alcohol.

JOSEPHINE
You know what Marie told me tonight?

MAEVE
No.

JOSEPHINE
She missed her period.

MAEVE
You mean?

JOSEPHINE
With Ben Hair.

MAEVE
Uh no! He's so dumb.

JOSEPHINE
I said, was she sure? She said, no, she isn't sure.

MAEVE
I hope not. But maybe she won't run away to Canada if she has a baby. Maybe that would be alright.

JOSEPHINE
There are ways to get rid of it, you know.

MAEVE
Really? How?

JOSEPHINE
I don't know, but I know they can do it. I've heard there is a doctor on the rez who does it. It's against the law but he's on the rez so it doesn't count.

MAEVE
You think Marie would do that? To her own baby?

JOSEPHINE
I don't know. But maybe it's better than being stuck around here, married to Ben Hair.

MAEVE
I want to have a baby.

JOSEPHINE
Don't say that.

MAEVE
It's true. Lots.

JOSEPHINE
You don't know anything about it. You don't even know how it works.

MAEVE
Sure I do.

JOSEPHINE
No, you don't. And you are too young anyway. Say, you're not fooling around with that boy, are you? What's his name?

MAEVE
Tyler.

JOSEPHINE
Tyler? What kind of name is that?

MAEVE
Bloodworth. He's Flathead Native. Works at the mine with Uncle
Lyle.

JOSEPHINE
You're fif-TEEN! You should not be hanging around with some
Flathead miner. How old is he?

MAEVE
Same as you. Just turned eighteen.

JOSEPHINE
Maeve, honey, you've got to stay away from him. He'll get you
pregnant faster than you can swivel your head.

MAEVE
He plays baseball in the summer. The Twins have invited him to go
out to the Cities in the spring for a tryout. He wants me to come with.

JOSEPHINE
Have you told Dad any of this, or were you just going to spring it on
him, or not tell him at all?

MAEVE
I don't mind staying here. I'll just go, see the Cities, then come back.

JOSEPHINE
I'm going to be eighteen next week and I want to start my life, get out
of this dusty place. But you are only fifteen. You have to finish
school, not get *in-trouble* with the first guy who talks sweet to you.
Use your head.

MAEVE
Are you going to go away?

JOSEPHINE
Probably. I need to go to Montreal or Quebec. That's where the
serious artists live. And with my talent and artistic vision, I really
have to be around other artists for my potential to really blossom. I
think that is best.

MAEVE
You could go to Helena. Or Denver?

JOSEPHINE
Cow-towns. I need to be in a place where there are art galleries and book publishers, so that my work has a place to live and breathe. The public will get to experience my genius, not just hear about some girl out West.

MAEVE
But you could paint here and mail them to Montreal.

JOSEPHINE
So much of the world of art, drama and criticism is built on relationships, at cocktail parties. That's what Georgia O'Keefe said. I need to be in the mix, in the mingle, in the marinade, of ideas.

MAEVE
Huh. OK. When do you leave?

JOSEPHINE
Oh, I don't have a train ticket just yet. And I need to hear about what's happening with Marie. If she's going to have a baby, I should be around to help.

MAEVE
Do you think she will have a baby, and marry Ben Hair?

JOSEPHINE
I don't know. We'll see next week. But I don't want you to have a baby either. Have you been seeing each other?

MAEVE
He was in town with Uncle Lyle. He introduced us. I met him at the ice-cream shop on Saturday and he wants to take me to the pictures this Wednesday.

JOSEPHINE
Maeve, no. Do not do this.

MAEVE
He's a sweet boy. He's smart and funny, and soooo cute!

JOSEPHINE
Guys like that are two-bits-a-dozen. Farmhands, miners, railroad fellas. You've got to aim higher. Find a boy who wants to be a teacher

or a lawyer. You're smart. You shouldn't have to fix your wagon to some roustabout, baseball or not.

MAEVE
But how am I going to find out about the world, if I don't find out about the world?

JOSEPHINE
Listen, I'll tell you anything you want to know.

MAEVE
But you don't even have a boyfriend. You don't know.

JOSEPHINE
Just because I haven't subjected myself to being pawed and groped by the whole football squad...

MAEVE
Like Susan Jennings!

JOSEPHINE
Like Susan Jennings, yes. Just because I haven't gone steady with any boys doesn't mean that I don't know my way around.

MAEVE
I don't believe you.

JOSEPHINE
Go ahead. I've spent many hours at the library, reading up on such matters. Ask me anything.

MAEVE
OK. Why do we girls get a period every month?

JOSEPHINE
Because the world is unfair and there is no justice for women. That's why. We just do.

MAEVE
Huh. OK. Where do babies come from?

JOSEPHINE
Same place as the period.

MAEVE
But, it's too small. That can't be.

JOSEPHINE
You've seen cows calving, out on the ranch. She gets with the bull
and then after a while the calf comes out. Same place.

MAEVE
That's gross.

JOSEPHINE
Kinda.

MAEVE
Why would you do that?

JOSEPHINE
I wouldn't.

MAEVE
But Marie does.

JOSEPHINE
Maybe. We'll see. Listen, if you're serious, you can bring, what's his
name?...

MAEVE
Tyler.

JOSEPHINE
You can bring Tyler to the party. But no hanky-panky. Got it?

MAEVE
Right, boss!

JOSEPHINE
Now go to bed. I'm going to clean up and read a little.

MAEVE
OK. Good night.

JOSEPHINE
Good night.

Maeve exits upstairs. Josephine clears up the glasses, replaces the whiskey bottle and sits down in the recliner with a book.

INT. - WAYNE'S BEDROOM - LATER

In the small bedroom, Wayne is asleep on a narrow double-bed. The ghost of his wife, IRENE, comes in and stands over him.

Wayne wakes up and notices her there.

IRENE
Wayne. Wake up.

WAYNE
Huh, what? Irene, what are you doing here?

IRENE
Wayne, what are you doing?

WAYNE
Trying to sleep. Go back to heaven.

IRENE
I will not go back to heaven. I mean, what are you doing about our girls? They are running wild and you are drunk and asleep. Do you even know what's going on, right under your nose?

WAYNE
They're good girls. I trust them.

IRENE
They are running around like whores in the street.

WAYNE
They are not.

IRENE
You have to take a firm hand with them. Show them that you won't take this kind of thing. They are turning into floozies.

WAYNE
They are good girls. They are smart.

IRENE

You need to use your belt on them. Particularly that Josie. She's a bad influence on our girls. Whip her, Wayne.

WAYNE
Irene, I'm not whipping anybody. Not Josie, not Maeve. I ought to turn you over my knee, is what I ought to do.

IRENE
I will not have you just sit by like a chewed-up plug of tobacco while Josie ruins my Maeve with her disgusting ideas. She wants Maeve to turn tricks in the street, for any Indian who honks. Do you realize that? Do you?

WAYNE
You don't know any of that, Irene.

IRENE
I know that you and your cripple brother just sit around getting drunk every night, while my girls turn into tramps. And you call yourself a father.

WAYNE
Reuben just comes by to visit. And you know he was a hero. He was injured in the war. Not just born deformed.

IRENE
Wayne, do you have any idea how filthy and dirty that Josie is? She doesn't wash her hair. She doesn't brush her teeth. She's like a horrible witch.

WAYNE
Irene, you're the ghost here. Why are you haunting me?

IRENE
They are playing you for a fool, Wayne. They always have. The people in town. That grain broker at the co-op, he plays you like a fiddle, cheats you every year. And you put up with it. If you had any guts you'd have shot him in the street. But you don't.

WAYNE
Prices are prices. I don't set 'em. Neither do you. We do alright with our grain. Why, it was a good solid crop this year. Both the rye and the millet all sold out. The whole crop.

IRENE

That's because you believed everything that snake told you and you gave away your year of work for a song. The next man in got twice as much. You look like a fool, Wayne. You are a fool.

WAYNE

I asked you a question: why are you haunting me?

IRENE

You think they don't know about you? They watch this place all the time. They see what's going on. There is probably a tap on the phone to keep tabs on you. They are listening all the time.

WAYNE

Who?

IRENE

Everybody. The town. The Indians. The priest. He's the worst, you know. He's been doing it with Maeve since she was twelve. Any you, you look the other way! Useless!

WAYNE

Cripes, Irene!

IRENE

You are going to end up turning this place into a whore house, taking money from any man who drives by. My girls, used like slaves, like breeding animals. Don't you see what's happening? Wayne, get control. Whip the girls.

WAYNE

No! No. Go back to the grave, Irene. Leave me alone. Leave me.

IRENE

You want to go to sleep but, right now, there could be a dozen men lined up to put their filthy hands up her skirt. Miners, field hands, Indian trappers. They only want one thing, young, white flesh. You'll go down in the morning and see the piles of dirty silver dollars.

WAYNE

Jesus, Irene. Leave me. Leave me in peace. Leave me.

IRENE

Wayne, you are a worthless failure, as a farmer and as a father.

Irene walks into a window and disappears.

WAYNE
(rattled)
Lord Jesus, please, let that woman rest in peace.

Wayne gets up, pulls on his trousers and goes out, downstairs.

INT. - KITCHEN - SAME TIME

Wayne comes down the stairs and goes to the kitchen. He fishes around for the whiskey bottle, noticing that it has been moved and the glasses have been moved. He looks over to see Josephine sitting in the front room reading.

Wayne pours a shot of whiskey, downs it, rinses the glass and puts everything back.

WAYNE
You still up?

JOSEPHINE
Just reading some.

WAYNE
Can I joins ya?

JOSEPHINE
Of course.

Wayne sits on a chair near Josephine.

WAYNE
Ya know, I'm real proud of you. You've done real well. I just want you to know that.

JOSEPHINE
Aww, thanks Dad.

WAYNE
And happy birthday, early.

JOSEPHINE
You're sweet.

WAYNE
What are you thinking about now, since you're done with school and such?

JOSEPHINE
You mean, when can you get me out of your hair?

WAYNE
Oh, I don't have much hair but I've got plenty for the bunch of us. You're no trouble.

JOSEPHINE
I know what you mean.

WAYNE
Like for after the holidays, the new year.

JOSEPHINE
1957.

WAYNE
Yup.

JOSEPHINE
Well, it's not official yet but I wrote away to some colleges.

WAYNE
Oh, have you?

JOSEPHINE
Yep.

WAYNE
Like M-T State?

JOSEPHINE
No, more like art school.

WAYNE
Oh. Is that right? Uh, where's that?

JOSEPHINE
Montreal.

WAYNE
Roy G Biv! Cripes. Montreal? Why all the way over there?

JOSEPHINE
Well, for one, it's free.

WAYNE
How's that?

JOSEPHINE
I sent them a portfolio and they offered a scholarship. I just have to get there.

WAYNE
Well, I'll be. Aren't you the one then? They send a letter, did they?

JOSEPHINE
I called them on the telephone and talked to the lady there. She said they sent a letter but she told me over the long-distance that I was in, and there was a scholarship attached to the offer.

WAYNE
Over long-distance, this was?

JOSEPHINE
Yep. Long-distance.

WAYNE
Why, can you beat that?

JOSEPHINE
Nope.

WAYNE
And when, you know, would you need to be there?

JOSEPHINE
First week of January.

WAYNE
Why that's only, what, six-seven weeks. Right after the Christmas.

Where would you stay?

JOSEPHINE
There is a student dormitory on Rue de Saint Marie. Isn't that lucky?
A street named after our Marie.

WAYNE
Oh, yeah. That's... that's a fine thing. Gosh, you're smart, Josie. I'm
real proud of ya.

JOSEPHINE
I'm going to miss you, Dad.

WAYNE
Oh, I hate to see you go. I wish you wouldn't.

JOSEPHINE
Dad?

WAYNE
But I'd hate it even more if you didn't go. No, you've picked your
path. Time to step into it.

JOSEPHINE
Thank you, Daddy. I love you.

WAYNE
Say, there's one thing, too. Uncle Reuben mentioned that he told
Marie he'd spot her five-hundred dollars if she was headed to the big
cities to get a job.

JOSEPHINE
Really?

WAYNE
Yup. And I don't see why he wouldn't put up the same for you as
well. I'll bend his ear on it. But keep an eye on him, would you?

JOSEPHINE
You betcha!

WAYNE
Right. My work is done here. I'm going back to bed. Goodnight love.

JOSEPHINE
Good night, Daddy. Sleep tight.

WAYNE
Sleep right.

Wayne exits. Josephine is thrilled.

INT. DAY - SATURDAY AFTERNOON - MAIN ROOM

It is the day of the party. People are spread out, chatting in the kitchen and the main room. BEN HAIR is there with Marie, and WIDOW RILEY is talking to MAEVE.

MAEVE
Well, I just have one more year left and then I'll be done with school.

WIDOW RILEY
Done with school? You are such a bright girl, you should go on to college.

MAEVE
I'm tired of school already. And besides, Marie didn't go to college and she's got a job, and a husband and a baby.

WIDOW RILEY
(shocked)
A baby? Who told you that?

MAEVE
Josie. She said it's not real sure yet though. But if she has a baby, maybe she and Ben Hair will get married and stay here.

WIDOW RILEY
Is she going away? She works at the bank.

MAEVE
She works at the bank but has read all about how she could get a job at a bigger bank, in Toronto.

WIDOW RILEY
Oh, yes. I remember her saying something about a better job but this is the first I have heard of moving away. Why Toronto?

MAEVE
I dunno. Maybe cause that's where they have big banks?

WIDOW RILEY
Maybe. I'll ask her. Say, are you excited about Josephine's birthday?

MAEVE
Uh-huh! And I get to bring in the cake!

WIDOW RILEY
Well then, you'd better get going.

MAEVE
I'm going to light the candles!

WIDOW RILEY
OK!

Maeve goes into the kitchen area and begins preparation for the cake.

WAYNE
(to Widow Riley)
Miss Riley, good of you to come today.

WIDOW RILEY
Wayne, how are you now?

WAYNE
On a daughter's birthday, why it's a reminder that I'm the luckiest
fella above ground.

WIDOW RILEY
Truly said, Wayne, truly said. And the birthday girl is in fine form, is
she?

WAYNE
That she is. In fact, a*nd this is just between you and me,* she received
in the mail today a letter from an art college. She's in.

WIDOW RILEY
That's marvelous! Good for her. When does she start?

WAYNE
First week of January. I'm thinking we'll ride up to Regina after

Christmas and she can take the new train all the way to Montreal.

WIDOW RILEY
Montreal? Oh my, that's so far.

WAYNE
Yep, it's a fer piece but they've got a line that goes all the way.
Regina, Winnipeg, Thunder Bay, Sudbury, then a leg over to
Montreal. I've looked her over and it's quite something that new
Canadian-line. Goes clear across, from the Atlantic to the Pacific.
Opened last year.

WIDOW RILEY
Goodness!

WAYNE
Right, well, I guess them Canadians had to catch up with us down
South, almost a hundred years later with a transcontinental rail line.
But a fine way to travel, I'd wager.

WIDOW RILEY
And Marie? Is she going too?

WAYNE
Well, I don't know about that. She's been dreaming big about heading
east and getting a big job at a big bank, in Toronto. But now Joe Hair
is holding her hand there so I don't know if she might stick around
this dusty place for a while longer.

WIDOW RILEY
Wayne, *just between us,* she's a smart girl. She can do better than Joe
Hair, don't you think?

WAYNE
She's grown now and can make her own decisions. If it is a Hair-boy
that's going to keep her around, well, by golly, I'd best keep my
mouth shut. But, frankly, I'd like to see her make her way in the wide
world before she gets too stuck-in here. Know what I mean?

WIDOW RILEY
I do.

WAYNE

Why it was Mister Riley done brought you round here, wasn't it?
Where were your people?

WIDOW RILEY
I have a sister in Rhode Island. That's where I grew up.

WAYNE
And your Mister Riley, how'd you two meet if you was back East?

WIDOW RILEY
Well, you knew Charles. Somehow he'd gotten the idea to join the
Navy during the war. A Montana man, so far from the ocean that he
said he couldn't even imagine how big it was. He was stationed at
Newport Naval Station, before he went to France. He was killed in
the invasion.

WAYNE
How'd you work in time to do any courtin', if you don't mind me
asking?

WIDOW RILEY
I was at a Catholic women's college nearby, *Salve Regina,* and the
nuns kept a close watch, you can believe me. But Friday night was
free and with the war-on, sailors filled the town. There were dances,
movies, suppers, lectures. It was a wonderful time, for me anyway.

WAYNE
I see.

WIDOW RILEY
And when Charley got news that they were going to ship out to the
war in Europe soon, he proposed. We were married that weekend.
The school term was ending so I got an apartment, for a month.
That's all I got with him, one month of May, 1944. Then he shipped
out.

WAYNE
And he got it on the beach, they said here in town.

WIDOW RILEY
I suppose so. We got an official report but it was all confusion and
shooting, so nobody is really sure what happened. And in the end, it
didn't matter. He was dead.

WAYNE
Charlie was a real character. He was a year ahead of me at school.
Him and my brother Lyle were friends. I think him and Charley
signed up together. He was Navy too, but Lyle ran the engine room in
one of them big gunboats. He doesn't talk about it much, on account
of what they seen, I guess.

WIDOW RILEY
Right. It's hard.

WAYNE
So, I mean, you're a good-looking gal. You didn't re-marry?

WIDOW RILEY
Kind of you to say that. No, I took the train that summer, through
Chicago and the Twin Cities, to see his mother. I stayed with her
while we waited for news. The War Department sent a letter saying
that he was buried in France but we could have his body sent back to
Montana if we wanted. As the wife of record, it was officially my
decision so I wrote Washington and told them to send him back to
Medicine Lake. Which they did, three years later.

WAYNE
Cripes!

WIDOW RILEY
By that time I'd been in Montana with his mother the whole time. She
had been so crushed by losing Charles that I felt I should look after
her. She was ill but still living for many years. So I got a job with
Sheridan County and lived with his mother until she passed.

WAYNE
Two year ago, was it?

WIDOW RILEY
Almost three now. A man arrived with Charley's body in forty-eight,
so we buried him in town, but I've been here for twelve years myself.

WAYNE
Well I know my brother Reuben has been asking about you. He was a
soldier too, you know.

WIDOW RILEY

Was he?

WAYNE
Army. Rode a tank into Paris. But he got shot-up in Germany and
was in the hospital for a while after that. It must have been something
because he left Montana with a buddy one day, and came back two-
and-a-half-years later a different man. His buddy didn't make it.

WIDOW RILEY
Does he live here, with you?

WAYNE
The other house on the property. Dad built it, thinking that, with three
boys, one of 'em would be a farmer and could take over for him but
have a place for a wife and a family here.

WIDOW RILEY
So he just lives alone in there?

WAYNE
Oh, we work the farm together, him and me. Then he goes to wash up
and sometimes comes down here for supper. The girls like him and
they get him all riled up. They are so smart, these girls.

WIDOW RILEY
You've done a good job with them. You have every reason to be
proud, as a father.

WAYNE
Thank you, Widow Riley.

WIDOW RILEY
And I must say that I didn't know Irene for long but she was such a
sweet person. And her twin sister, my word! They were just hilarious
when they were together. Talking so fast and laughing, making
everybody laugh. Oh my, oh my! I remember one time, I went
skating with them. It was so cold but we laughed and laughed. They
were such good skaters too. That's why it was so strange at the end.
Oh, I'm sorry, Wayne. I shouldn't have brought it up.

WAYNE
The both of us have lost, and suffered. No denying it. But it is a day
for joyful thoughts, for Josephine.

WIDOW RILEY
But you, Wayne, you never re-married?

WAYNE
Oh, with three girls, I've got more than my hands full. But I do worry that Reuben's house is awfully cold. He's never been much of the ladies-man.

WIDOW RILEY
What are you suggesting?

WAYNE
I think it would be a nice thing for him to have some companionship. And if you two were to make a thing of things, I wouldn't stand in the way of that.

WIDOW RILEY
(chuckling)
So I have your blessings?

WAYNE
So you do. I don't know of another lady round here that I'd trust with my own brother. 'Cept you.

WIDOW RILEY
Thank you, Wayne. But what is his feeling on the matter?

WAYNE
I've been the little bird on his shoulder, saying he should pay attention to such matters. But I will say, he might need a kick in the pants.

WIDOW RILEY
(laughs)
Doctors' Orders?

WAYNE
Something like that. Speaking of...
(to Reuben)
Roob! Come here now.

REUBEN
(nods)

Wayne. Widow Riley. Good to see you today? Can I get you something?

WIDOW RILEY
I'd like something stiff.

REUBEN
Um, drinks then?

WAYNE
A drop of rye would suit ya?

WIDOW RILEY
Very nice. With a splash of water.

WAYNE
I'll fetch it. And one for you, Roob.

Wayne exits to get drinks.

WIDOW RILEY
Wayne tells me that you farm with him here.

REUBEN
That's right. Pretty much spent my whole life planted right here.

WIDOW RILEY
But he said you were in the war.

REUBEN
I don't like to talk too much about it. Lotta hard times then.

WIDOW RILEY
My Charley was in France. Killed in Action.

REUBEN
K-I-A, that's what they called it. I was lucky to get out with just getting shot all to pieces. By the time I got back I didn't ever want to see the inside of a hospital again. And, aside from when Mother passed, it's been that way.

WIDOW RILEY
I see.

REUBEN
I remember Charly. Charles Riley. Him and my brother Lyle were two years behind me at school. He could throw a baseball harder than any man I've ever seen. He was that good. Then they went into the Navy together.

WIDOW RILEY
That's right. It seems like yesterday.

REUBEN
Or a million lifetimes ago.

WIDOW RILEY
Yes. Like it all happened to somebody else.

REUBEN
But I remember Charley. His mother was a sweet lady. You moved in with her then, didn't you?

WIDOW RILEY
It was so hard on her when Charley died that I just stayed with her for a while, and here I am, a dozen years later.

REUBEN
Why have you not re-married then?

WIDOW RILEY
I talked to my sister on the telephone recently and she asked me the same thing. I told her, *the odds-are-good, but the goods-are-odd!*

REUBEN
Oh. Well, I stick to myself mostly.

WIDOW RILEY
Well, what I mean is that there is not much to interest an older woman here.

REUBEN
I see.

WIDOW RILEY
Excepting yourself, though. Did you see Paris?

REUBEN
(laughs)
Oh, long time ago. It was pretty though. Beautiful river. Castles.
Amazing.

WIDOW RILEY
Reuben, I don't want to be too forward, but how about you come into
town for dinner at my house this week? It will be a nice change to
have some company.

REUBEN
Well, I don't get out much, I suppose.

WIDOW RILEY
This will be a chance. We could cook some steaks. And some
potatoes.

REUBEN
Well, sure, ya. I could bring some down to you. We've got plenty of
prime cuts at the locker. Bring a dozen, say?

WIDOW RILEY
A dozen? I don't think we can eat all that.

REUBEN
Sure, ya, but you can keep them in the ice box. I mean, you can't
really buy good meat around here, even though we got steaks on-the-
hoof right outside this window.

WIDOW RILEY
Maybe I could come by your place, tomorrow and visit as well.

REUBEN
Well, there was talk of Lyle and me going fishing.

WIDOW RILEY
I see.

REUBEN
But I'll wave him off. The fish aren't going anywhere.

WIDOW RILEY
I'd like that, Reuben.

REUBEN
Give me a little time to clean up, I guess.

WIDOW RILEY
I'll come by mid-morning, if that works for you.

REUBEN
Sure, ya.

WIDOW RILEY
Say, what do you think of Marie?

REUBEN
How do you mean? She's smart as a whip and almost as pretty as her mother.

WIDOW RILEY
But Ben Hair?

REUBEN
Ah, jeez. The Hair boys, Mother used to say, aren't smart enough to play cards.

WIDOW RILEY
(laughs)
Oh-ho! That's a good one. Yes, I don't see them lasting long. But is there anything else holding them together?

REUBEN
Just two love-birds, I'd say. I don't know much about it.

WIDOW RILEY
That's probably it.

Wayne arrives with drinks.

WAYNE
Here you go now.

WIDOW RILEY
Thanks, Wayne.

WAYNE
Sure, and let me peel you away from the clutches of my brother. I'd

like you to talk to Marie.

WIDOW RILEY
See you tomorrow then, Reuben.

REUBEN
Right-o!

They move across the room to meet Marie and Ben.

WAYNE
Marie, you know the Widow Riley, don't ya?

MARIE
Hello, Missus Riley. You look lovely today.

WIDOW RILEY
Oh, thank you, Marie. Any excuse for a dress up.

WAYNE
(to Ben)
Ben, can I grab you a minute? We're going to sing the birthday song in a minute, and I want to get a few fellas together to practice a few bars.

Wayne pulls Ben away and walks him out a side door. He signals to Reuben, who follows them out.

WIDOW RILEY
I keep hearing that you are coming up on a promotion of some kind. Are you taking a new job?

MARIE
I thought so. But now, I don't know.

WIDOW RILEY
What's happened?

MARIE
Well, with Ben and all, maybe I should stay here.

WIDOW RILEY
I heard you mentioned Toronto. Why Canada?

MARIE
I just want to get out of this little crossroads of a town.

WIDOW RILEY
And the bank?

MARIE
They have an office in Toronto and I can slot right in, they said.

WIDOW RILEY
So what's holding you back? Ben doesn't want you to go?

MARIE
It's that and..

WIDOW RILEY
(softly, close-in)
Marie, tell me the truth, are you pregnant?

MARIE
(nods)
Mmm-hmm. I think so.

WIDOW RILEY
How far along?

MARIE
Maybe six weeks.

WIDOW RILEY
I can help you. If you want.

MARIE
I don't know what I want.

WIDOW RILEY
I have helped girls, in your condition, before. If you want, it's safe.

MARIE
My dad would kill me if I did that.

WIDOW RILEY
We'll see about that. And Ben, does he know?

MARIE
I haven't told him.

WIDOW RILEY
(nods)
Look, I know that you don't really know me or have any reason to trust me but I can help you. But you have to decide soon. If it goes too long, then you can't. Or if you want to give the baby up, I can work with you on that too. I work for the county, in the areas that you need. I'm here to help.

MARIE
(nervous)
OK.

WIDOW RILEY
You think about it and we can talk about it tomorrow. I'm coming by to visit Reuben in the morning.

MARIE
Wait. You. And Uncle Reuben? But you're so pretty!

WIDOW RILEY
Thank you dear. But, honestly, the nights get cold.

MARIE
Wow. Uh, OK.

WIDOW RILEY
So let's talk tomorrow and we'll make a plan.

MARIE
Ok. Thank you. I don't have anybody to talk to about this.

WIDOW RILEY
I know. But I'm here.

Wayne enters, with Ben and Reuben.

WAYNE
Seems like we ought to get the party started. Where's the star of the show?

Josephine is with a group of her friends. She breaks away for the party.

JOSEPHINE
Dad! You don't have to make a big show.

WAYNE
We sure do, darling.
(to the party)
Folks, listen up for a moment. I just want to say how nice it is to have all you folks here today for Josie's birthday. She's eighteen today so set back the phone-poles because this little girl is going to be blazing a trail.

JOSEPHINE
Oh, Dad.

WAYNE
And folks, here's a gift that every parent loves to give, and that's a letter from the Academy of Fine Arts in Montreal, with an announcement of acceptance and a scholarship to go there. Congratulations, Josie!

JOSEPHINE
(hugs Wayne)
Oh, Dad! You don't have to make a big deal about it.

WAYNE
I certainly do, sweetie. I am over the moon for you.
(kisses her)

JOSEPHINE
I love you, papa.

WAYNE
I love you too, kid. Now let's bring out the cake and sing!

Maeve picks up a box of Canadian Rail matches, made of cedar, and lights candles for the cake. She brings in the flaming cake and sets it on the table.

Everybody gathers around Josephine and the cake.

WAYNE

(singing, everyone joins)
Happy Birthday to you!
Happy Birthday to you!
Happy Birth-day dear Josie!
Happy Birth-day to you!

ALL
Hurray! Blow out the candles! Make a wish!

JOSEPHINE
Thank you, all!

She blows out the candles. People clap.

WAYNE
OK, step right up. First the birthday girl.

Wayne cuts cake for Josephine, Maeve and Marie. People eat cake, pour drinks and kiss Josephine. Party.

INT. - FARMHOUSE FRONT ROOM - LATER

Wayne and Reuben are relaxing after the party. There is a bottle of rye whiskey on the table in front of them.

REUBEN
Such a fun time, Wayne.

WAYNE
Turned out all right.

REUBEN
She's a solid girl.

WAYNE
Right as rain.

REUBEN
Be a shame to see her go.

WAYNE
Be a shame if she stayed around this hick town.

REUBEN

Cleverest person in the room

WAYNE
I don't know about that. The Widow is a sharp one. And nice ankles too, I'd note.

REUBEN
Yeah, not sure what's gotten into her but she's coming by tomorrow. And then we're going to have steaks at her place later this week. Reminds me, I've got to swing by the Locker and pick up a dozen.

WAYNE
Cripes! A dozen steaks? You going to choke her with 'em?

REUBEN
No, for the ice-box, I told her.

WAYNE
Oh, right. Makes sense.

REUBEN
A good time. Oh, to be young again.

WAYNE
I wouldn't want to go through it again.

REUBEN
You mean the war?

WAYNE
No, just in general, being young. Why look at the Hair boy. He knows he's not half good enough for Marie. One look and you know he's about to get the boot. I remember feeling that way with Irene.

REUBEN
Do ya?

WAYNE
She stuck by me, though. Lord knows why.

REUBEN
There's no explaining a woman's heart.

WAYNE

Yep.

REUBEN
Nothing for it, I suppose.

WAYNE
I suppose.

REUBEN
Why that Widow Riley though, she reminds me of somebody.

WAYNE
Who'd that be then?

REUBEN
During the war, ya know, I was stationed in England for training.

WAYNE
Was there a nurse or someone?

REUBEN
Local girl, from Sheffield. She was a volunteer and worked in the staff office.

WAYNE
A secretary, like?

REUBEN
I guess. She didn't say too much about it but we kinda hit it off and we went to the pictures.

WAYNE
And what was her name?

REUBEN
Claire. Ecclestone.

WAYNE
So... did ya...?

REUBEN
Kiss her, you mean?

WAYNE

Well, OK, ya. Did you get to kiss her?

REUBEN
I did.

WAYNE
So, how'd that go, then?

REUBEN
Well, I'm telling you, aren't I, so I guess I remember it pretty fondly.

WAYNE
Sounds like. Did you write to her? Know what become of her?

REUBEN
Oh, I got shipped out, then got shot up. I wasn't but a few years older than Josie is today. But I was thinking about it, her, what with all the women around about for the party. Don't see that many women, all in one place, too much. Just made me think about what it might have been like, her and me.

WAYNE
Living there, you mean?

REUBEN
Me there, or her here. Which do you think would have taken hold?

WAYNE
Oh, I'd imagine you'd a made a good show of her either way. Seems a shame not to take a swing at it, you know, on account of life being funny like that.

REUBEN
I don't reckon it would have been right to bring her back here. Nothing here for a woman like that. Smart, pretty, sophisticated. Just not enough around, is what I'm saying.

WAYNE
Well, now my Irene, she was smart as could be, and you said yourself that she was as fair as they come. She dug in here, married, children. The whole shebang.

REUBEN

But she had her sister too, you know.

WAYNE
Well that's right. Both or none with them two. So you would've been an English farmer then? Wet sheep and rocks?

REUBEN
Oh, you should have seen it, Wayne. Green fields as far as you could see. Hedges, stone walls, soft green grass. Lovely place. Not like the hard grip here, with grass like sawblades and a wildfire if you're not looking, then freeze into a block come winter. Here, it's like nature is trying to kill you. There, it's like nature wants to help you along.

WAYNE
Quite the place.

REUBEN
And France was even more pretty, if you can believe it. The vineyards and the pretty towns. Shame you missed it, Wayne.

WAYNE
Probably still there. Maybe I'll take Maeve someday.

REUBEN
Or the Widow Riley.

WAYNE
Hey now, that's up your line. I've got my hands full.

REUBEN
Wayne, I've been shot up real good. I can't satisfy a woman like that anymore. It's not fair to her.

WAYNE
You talk like you are the ghost. Still got a beating heart don't ya? Well, sure you do. And about the worst way of living in the world is to go to sleep, alone in a cold bed.

REUBEN
And for you, yourself, Wayne!

WAYNE
I'm just glad for a night of peace.

REUBEN
So ya says. A bump then?
(indicates whiskey)

WAYNE
Nope. Say, I'm going up. You relax and I'll see ya tomorrow.

REUBEN
Sure enough then.

Wayne exits upstairs to his bedroom

Reuben sips the whiskey and is soon asleep in the chair.

INT. WAYNE'S BEDROOM - LATER

Wayne is asleep.

Ghost of IRENE enters.

IRENE
Wayne. Wake up.

WAYNE
Hmmgh?

IRENE
Wake up!

WAYNE
Irene, not again. Go to sleep, dear.

IRENE
I will not go to sleep when you are destroying our home. Those scheming tramps are planning on turning this house into some kind of dancing hall.

WAYNE
(confused)
A what? What are you saying?

IRENE
The minute you turn your back, those girls are going to have their boyfriends moving in here, with boarders. There will be god-knows

how many people loitering around here, all swapping sex, and drugs! There will be police coming by at all hours of the night. Our girls will be used-up hags by the time Maeve is twenty. And look at you!

WAYNE
Irene, please! Let me sleep. Go away. The girls are fine. They are nice girls.

IRENE
And your imbecile-cripple brother. That dummy is going to get his whole life flushed down the drain by that widow. And you invited her? Into MY home? This place will never lose the stink of her. She's been scheming to get her hands on your farm since she got to town. She's coming for you, Wayne! She's coming for you!
AAAAAAYYYYYYYEEEEEEEEE!!!
AAAAAAAAAYYYYYEEEE!!!

Irene flies around the room, shrieking at Wayne. Terrified Wayne jumps out of bed and runs out the door.

WAYNE
Get away from me! Get away! Irene!

IRENE
AAAAYYYYYYEEEEE!

Wayne bolts down the steps into the front room.

Reuben is awakened by Wayne's shouts. He sees Wayne running, waving his arms and seeing him run out into the cold night.

REUBEN
Wayne?!

Reuben jumps up and runs out the door after Wayne, closing the door.

INT. - NIGHT-   FRONT ROOM - LATER

Maeve and Josephine come in the door after the big night out.

JOSEPHINE
I'm beat.

MAEVE

That was so much fun.

JOSEPHINE
Where's Dad?

MAEVE
He must have gone up to bed.

JOSEPHINE
Uncle Reuben too.

MAEVE
Happy birthday, Josie.

JOSEPHINE
Thanks, M. Good night.

MAEVE
Bed time.

The two women go upstairs, each to their separate bedrooms.

INT. DAY - SATURDAY MORNING

Front room of the house. Maeve and Josephine are up.

MAEVE
Did you hear Dad get up?

JOSEPHINE
No, I haven't seen him.

MAEVE
I'm going to go check.

Maeve goes up the stairs.

WIDOW RILEY
(enters)
Good morning, birthday girl!

JOSEPHINE
Missus Riley, we can't find Dad.

WIDOW RILEY
He can't have gone far, his truck is there.

MAEVE
(comes downstairs)
He's not there. His trousers are there but he's not there.

WIDOW RILEY
I'll check with Reuben.
(exits)

JOSEPHINE
That's not like him. I wonder what happened.

MAEVE
Maybe him and Uncle Reuben had a fight. Maybe they killed each other.

JOSEPHINE
Or fell down and froze in the field.

MAEVE
Oh my god, maybe we're orphans.

JOSEPHINE
I am an orphan.

MAEVE
Now maybe we are all orphans. Now the cycle is complete!

JOSEPHINE
They can't be dead. We just saw them last night.

WIDOW RILEY
(returns)
Reuben is not there either.

JOSEPHINE
What do we do? Should we form a search party?

WIDOW RILEY
Where would they go?

MAEVE

Maybe they fell in the creek and both drown?

WIDOW RILEY
Let's have a look around the place. If we don't find them, we'll call the sheriff.

JOSEPHINE
Maeve, you go check the machine shed. I'll check the barn. Missus Riley, you'd better stay here, in case they show up.

WIDOW RILEY
Ok. I'll stay here.

Josephine and Maeve head out, searching.

Widow Riley sits down at the kitchen table, then gets up and makes some coffee. While she's waiting she looks around the place, having the whole place alone for once. She looks at a picture of young Irene with Wayne. There is a picture of young Josephine and Colleen. Then she pours a cup of coffee and waits. From outside, she hears Josephine.

JOSEPHINE
(outside)
Found 'em!

Wayne walks in the door. He is covered in dirt and is not wearing trousers or shoes. He is very cold. Reuben follows Wayne in. He is dressed as when he left at night but with no shoes.

WAYNE
Cripes! It's cold.

WIDOW RILEY
Wayne! Reuben! Here. Here's some hot coffee. Josie, get some blankets for them.

The two men come in and sit down, warmed by the coffee and blankets.

WAYNE
Roy G Biv.

WIDOW RILEY
What in the world happened?

137

REUBEN
I woke up in a ditch. It was still dark. I made it back to the machine shed.

WAYNE
By the time I come to, I was flat on my back in the barley field. All I remember was a terrible dream and I had to get out. I started running, in the dark, just to get away. I made it to the shed and found Roob.

REUBEN
Wayne found an old horse blanket and we put that over us 'til it was light. We were fixing to come in when we heard the girls.

WIDOW RILEY
My word! Are you alright? Are you hurt?

WAYNE
I must have gone teapot-over-kettle out in the field but nothing broken. I best go back up to bed for a while. You too Roob.

WIDOW RILEY
I'll see to him.

Reuben and Widow Riley exit to his house on the property.

JOSEPHINE
That's so strange!

MAEVE
(quietly)
Jo, do you think Dad is going crazy? He's been acting weird.

JOSEPHINE
Maybe. That was kinda crazy. I'll be glad to get to Montreal.

MAEVE
But don't leave me like this!

JOSEPHINE
No, I mean, when it's the right time to leave and everything is normal.

Marie enters.

MARIE

Hey birthday girl! That was sure fun last night.

MAEVE
Marie, you won't believe it!

MARIE
What?

JOSEPHINE
Dad and Uncle Rueben just walked in, from outside. They spent the
whole night outside.

MARIE
But it was near freezing last night!

MAEVE
Dad said he was having a bad dream and he had get out.

JOSEPHINE
And I guess Uncle Reuben followed him out.

MARIE
Oh no. I know what this is. It's Mom.

JOSEPHINE
Mom?

MARIE
Our mom, not your mom.

JOSEPHINE
Aunt Irene?

MARIE
Mom's ghost is haunting Dad. He told me one time.

MAEVE
So, the house is haunted!

JOSEPHINE
Aunt Irene is haunting Dad, from the dead?

MARIE
That's what he said. He told me, Mom appears in his bedroom and

yells at him. He said she's mean and sad, not like she was in real life.

MAEVE
How come I never get to see her ghost?

MARIE
I think because Dad is dreaming it. She's not real.

MAEVE
But maybe ghosts are real.

MARIE
Maybe. Did I see Missus Riley's car outside?

JOSEPHINE
Yes. She took Reuben back to his house.

MARIE
Oh? Are they...?

JOSEPHINE
I don't know. Maybe.

MAEVE
I think Dad was trying to set them up. Hey, Marie, are you going to have a baby?

MARIE
Would you pipe down! I don't want Dad to hear.

MAEVE
Don't worry, all he can hear is Mom yelling at him. So?

MARIE
I'm going to talk to Missus Riley about it. She says she can help.

JOSEPHINE
Marie, maybe you could come to Canada with me.

MARIE
What do you mean?

JOSEPHINE
I'm taking the train and it's a real long way. We go through Toronto.

Maybe we go together.

MARIE
Oh, I can't even think about that right now! Where is she?

JOSEPHINE
Maybe you should go over and talk to her. I bet she put Uncle Reuben to bed. They were both just about frozen.

MARIE
How weird!

MAEVE
Dad was all dirty too. He said he fell down in the barley field.

MARIE
Maybe you are right. I'll go talk to her.

Marie exits and goes to Reuben's house.

Josephine pours herself some coffee. Both sit down.

JOSEPHINE
This is so weird.

MAEVE
Should we do something?

JOSEPHINE
I don't know. He seems all right, I guess.

MAEVE
We'll see how he is later.

JOSEPHINE
The thing is...

MAEVE
What?

JOSEPHINE
If Dad is going crazy, then he won't be able to take care of you.

MAEVE

What do you mean?

JOSEPHINE
If Marie is serious about going to Toronto, and Dad goes insane, then, as a real grown-up, I think you become my responsibility.

MAEVE
Do I have to call you Mom?

JOSEPHINE
It's not like that. It's like, I don't know, like, I have to adopt you or something, until you turn eighteen.

MAEVE
That would be weird. I'll have to learn French.

JOSEPHINE
Why?

MAEVE
Because I'll have to come to Montreal with you, on account of you being my legal whatever.

JOSEPHINE
I can't go to Montreal if I'm responsible for you. Maybe Marie can get me a job at the bank.

MAEVE
Or you could take up the farming?

JOSEPHINE
Me? Farming?

MAEVE
Or you could marry a farmer, like Marie and Joe Hair.

JOSEPHINE
Joe is no farmer. He works at the mine with Uncle Lyle and your Tayler.

MAEVE
Tyler. He wants to farm. He says he hates the mine and wants to have some property, to work the land.

JOSEPHINE
(scoffs)
Work the land. He doesn't know the first thing about farming. The
Flatheads were buffalo hunters, not farmers.

MAEVE
Tyler grew up on a farm. His brothers work on their dad's farm, north
of Plentywood. Tyler took the mining job because he was the
youngest.

JOSEPHINE
So what are you saying? You want to have Taylor come over and
farm with Dad?

MAEVE
Well, he's nearly eighteen so maybe he could be my legal thing.

JOSEPHINE
That would be a husband. You're moving pretty fast there, girlie.

MAEVE
But if Dad goes crazy and you and Marie move to Canada...
(starts to cry)

JOSEPHINE
Hey, hey now. It's not as bad as all that. It's going to be OK. Dad's
just upstairs sleeping it off. Probably just too much cake, is all.

MAEVE
(crying)
But what if he's dead? What if Mom killed him?

JOSEPHINE
Maeve, honey. Put on your big-girl pants. Get a hold of yourself.
You've got to think straight.

MAEVE
But I'm only fifteen!

JOSEPHINE
I know, I know. It's alright.

MAEVE

And what if Tyler goes to the baseball and all the women throw their *hussy-selves* at him? What then? He'll leave me behind too. And I'll be all by myself.

JOSEPHINE
Maeve, I won't leave you. If Dad dies, I'll stay here.

MAEVE
But you have your art to do, with the famous people in Canada.

JOSEPHINE
I will send them my art by parcel post.

MAEVE
But you'd hate me if you stayed here.

JOSEPHINE
It would only be until you turned eighteen. Then you are out the door, little lady.

MAEVE
Really?

JOSEPHINE
I don't know. Dad will be fine.

MAEVE
You really think so.

JOSEPHINE
I don't know but I think you have to do some thinking about what you want and how to get it. I worked in the grocery store when I was sixteen, after school. Then I got the full-time job at the meat-locker. If I can get those jobs, so can you. Then you can make your own money and look out for yourself.

MAEVE
But how?

JOSEPHINE
I'll talk to Joe Kobloisie, see if you can get the part-time job at the grocery. Maybe start before the holidays. He always needs help then.

MAEVE
Do you think I could do it?

JOSEPHINE
No.

MAEVE
No?

JOSEPHINE
(laughs)
But you'll learn. Stacking-and-stocking, that's most of it.

MAEVE
Ok, if you'll help.

JOSEPHINE
I'll help.

They hug.

INT. KITCHEN - EVENING

Wayne and Widow Riley are sitting down at the kitchen table.

WAYNE
Can I pour you one?

WIDOW RILEY
A short one. I should head home.

Wayne sets up glasses and a bottle of whiskey.

*W*AYNE
It was a nice thing you done to help Reuben.

WIDOW RILEY
I hate to see him so exhausted. What in the world happened?

WAYNE
Well I don't like to speak about it but I guess it's good to get it out.

WIDOW RILEY
Tell me, Wayne.

WAYNE
My wife, Irene, she comes into the bedroom when I'm asleep. She
wakes me up and says terrible things. Mean, cruel things. I don't
understand it at all.

WIDOW RILEY
You mean her ghost, her spirit visits you?

WAYNE
I don't know. I see her. I hear her. But I don't know.

WIDOW RILEY
I see.

WAYNE
And last night she was on me about the girls. She started screaming
and shrieking, this terrible sound. I got so scared I just started running
out the door. Like a damned fool.

WIDOW RILEY
Have you seen her any other place, like outside? In town?

WAYNE
Nope. Just here.

WIDOW RILEY
So maybe it's just a dream.

WAYNE
A hell of a dream then.

WIDOW RILEY
Wayne, there is something else we should talk about. Marie.

WAYNE
Marie? What is it?

WIDOW RILEY
I think you know.

WAYNE
Her and that damned Joe Hair boy?

WIDOW RILEY

Yes.

WAYNE
And is she, in trouble?

WIDOW RILEY
Possibly.

WAYNE
Dammit. I was thinking she was acting strange.

WIDOW RILEY
She's afraid to talk to you about it but I wanted to let you know.

WAYNE
I suppose she's going to have to marry that idiot now.

WIDOW RILEY
Not necessarily.

WAYNE
What are you talking about there?

WIDOW RILEY
There are a couple of options.

WAYNE
What options?

WIDOW RILEY
Well, let's go through them. First, what if they get married and have a baby? Is that so bad?

WAYNE
Where would they live? What would they do?

WIDOW RILEY
What if Rueben moved over here and Marie moved in there?

WAYNE
Hmmm. That's an option. I don't like it but it would be a thing we could do. What next?

WIDOW RILEY

Next, what if she had the baby and gave it up for adoption? The baby would be half Native and would qualify to live on the rez with a family that couldn't have children.

WAYNE
I don't like that one either. I couldn't think of there being a Webster son or daughter, just out on the reservation with some other family.

WIDOW RILEY
But it is an option.

WAYNE
It is an option. Again, I don't like it but it is an option.

WIDOW RILEY
Last is to end the pregnancy.

WAYNE
Kill the baby, you mean?

WIDOW RILEY
It's not a baby yet, Wayne. But it will be if she waits much longer.

WAYNE
That would be a terrible thing, wouldn't it?

WIDOW RILEY
But it is an option.

WAYNE
It's against the damned law!

WIDOW RILEY
Wayne, I work for Sheridan County and I deal with all kinds of services. I know a clinic on the reservation that handles these things, safely, legally. It is Native law on the rez, so they have a safe option. And I have seen too many young women panic and end up butchered by back-alley people. I don't want Marie to feel like she has to hide and panic. And you don't either.

WAYNE
No. I don't. I'd want her to talk to me about it.

WIDOW RILEY
But remember, she's twenty-two. She's her own woman. She's going to make the decision for herself. But, Wayne, she's scared and she is afraid you will be mad at her and ashamed of her.

WAYNE
Well, I am mad. And I am ashamed of her.

WIDOW RILEY
This is the hard part now. This is where we have to be adults and think about what is the right, and best, decision.

WAYNE
If you say so.

WIDOW RILEY
Do you think she loves him?

WAYNE
I don't see how. He's dumber than a box of rocks.

WIDOW RILEY
Why do you think she got involved with him? She's a smart girl.

WAYNE
Apparently not. And I don't know. The mind of a woman is a mystery.

WIDOW RILEY
We're just people.

WAYNE
I know. And I appreciate you talking this out with me. What's the plan?

WIDOW RILEY
I'm going to take Marie to the clinic tomorrow. They will talk to her about the options and she'll decide.

WAYNE
And the Hair-boy? Does he get a say?

WIDOW RILEY

That's between them.

WAYNE
A kettle of fish.

WIDOW RILEY
I will stop-in and check on Reuben tomorrow.

WAYNE
Widow Riley, could I impose on you to stay with him for the night? I don't know what the accommodations are but I'm worried about him dying all alone.

WIDOW RILEY
I am too. He looks awfully weak.

WAYNE
He meant to look after me, the younger brother. I was out of my mind and he wanted to save me. Didn't think of himself, just took off after me.

WIDOW RILEY
He's a brave man.

WAYNE
And I led him to the door of the dead.

WIDOW RILEY
Don't blame yourself.

WAYNE
Could you find a way to stay with him, see if he pulls through? Just for the night?

WIDOW RILEY
OK. Yes. I'll work it out. See you in the morning.

WAYNE
Good night. And thank you.

WIDOW RILEY
Good night, Wayne.

INT - FARMHOUSE FRONT ROOM - NEXT DAY - LATE

AFTERNOON

Wayne is eating a sandwich. Josie is drawing him on a pad of paper.

JOSEPHINE
You are moving too much.

WAYNE
Should I chew slower?

JOSEPHINE
No, just like that.

WAYNE
Still, you mean.

JOSEPHINE
Right.

WAYNE
How can I finish my sandwich?

JOSEPHINE
I want to have the sandwich details, so don't eat it all.

WAYNE
You artists. Funny birds. Why are you drawing me anyway?

JOSEPHINE
I want to have a picture I can hang on my wall in art school. A picture from here.

WAYNE
You should go outside and draw the fields or something.

JOSEPHINE
It would just be a straight line, "Horizon, Sky!"

WAYNE
(laughs)
I guess that's right. Say, when you're done there, would you be a pal and go check on Reuben?

JOSEPHINE

Sure, just a minute more.

WAYNE
Maybe take him a glass of milk.

JOSEPHINE
Doesn't he have milk?

WAYNE
I don't know. I haven't been in that place in, oh, three or four years now. I just feel strange going in there.

JOSEPHINE
I've been in there. It's alright. No plants or anything pretty, but it's alright, I guess.

WAYNE
I suppose. Say, tell me what it's going to be like at art college? How's it going to be?

JOSEPHINE
Oh, I think the curriculum will be full of drawing and painting, nude modelling, sculptures, that sort of thing.

WAYNE
Nude what?

JOSEPHINE
It's called 'figure studies'.

WAYNE
Why's that?

JOSEPHINE
Because you study the figure.

WAYNE
In the nude?

JOSEPHINE
Not the artist.

WAYNE
The model, then.

JOSEPHINE
Right. You draw a naked man and see all the details and proportions.

WAYNE
See all the details? That doesn't sound proper. For a lady.

JOSEPHINE
An artist has to explore the form of the body, the shape of the figure, the details - from the hands and feet to the hair on his head. I suppose they will use a whole lot of models.

WAYNE
Change them up, the men? Rotate 'em.

JOSEPHINE
I don't see why not. An artist has to be challenged with a new body, a new volume of space and motion.

WAYNE
You been reading all of this?

JOSEPHINE
Mmm-hmm. Georgia O'Keefe says that women have a special responsibility in art to fill the spaces with beauty.

WAYNE
Well, if it means anything to you, I want to let you know that you, and the other girls, are the luckiest thing that ever happened to me. You fill my life with beauty. Now I want you to go to art college and learn to fill the whole world with your beauty.

JOSEPHINE
Awww! Thanks Dad.

WAYNE
Now I've got to eat this sandwich and you have to go check on Reuben. Go.

JOSEPHINE
(puts down pencil)
OK.

She gets up and goes out to check on Reuben.

Wayne finishes his sandwich.

Outside, Widow Riley's car pulls up.

Marie and Maeve come in, followed by Riley.

WAYNE
Ladies.

MARIE
Dad, we went to see the clinic. But we're back.

WAYNE
I can see that. What are you thinking?

MARIE
I don't know.

WIDOW RILEY
Marie, go ahead.

MARIE
Daddy, I want to keep the baby.

WAYNE
And marry that dummy Joe Hair? Cripes!

MARIE
No, not marry Joe. Do this myself. He's already running around and I think he has a Native girlfriend already.

WAYNE
Another girl?

MARIE
They were together before, I think, and got back together. Anyway, I want to do this myself.

WAYNE
How's that going to work then?

MARIE
I can keep my job at the bank but, Daddy...

WAYNE
Go on.

MARIE
I think I need to move back home.

WAYNE
I been thinking about that.

MARIE
And?

WAYNE
Maybe that's for the best. We'll see how Reuben feels but the Widow Riley here suggested that he move in here, and you might have more space over there.

MARIE
In Uncle Reuben's house? Oh, my.

WAYNE
We'll just see how she goes. What else did the doctor say?

WIDOW RILEY
They were very helpful, very professional. They said everything looks normal. She's healthy and shouldn't have any trouble.

WAYNE
That's good to hear.

WIDOW RILEY
And there is another option as well.

WAYNE
Go on.

WIDOW RILEY
What if Maeve moves over into the house with Marie, for the time?

WAYNE
So it would be just Reuben and me then?

WIDOW RILEY
(sly)

Well, I'm not far.

WAYNE
Is that right?

WIDOW RILEY
We'll see how she goes, like you said.

MAEVE
Could I, Dad?

WAYNE
Things are moving fast here.

Josephine enters. She is ashen-faced, stunned.

JOSEPHINE
Daddy, I think Uncle Reuben might be dead.

WAYNE
Ah no. I blame myself.

WIDOW RILEY
Oh dear!

JOSEPHINE
He was just cold. And didn't move.

WIDOW RILEY
I'll go take a look.

WAYNE
No, he's my brother. I'll do it.

WIDOW RILEY
We'll do it together.

Wayne and Widow Riley go out the door.

Marie goes over to hug Josephine.

MARIE
You shouldn't have to see that.

JOSEPHINE
He was so cold. He didn't move or even blink.

Maeve comes over and hugs them both. All three hug together.

INT. FRONT ROOM - AFTERNOON - SUMMER

Wayne and Widow Riley are playing cards with a cribbage board.

WIDOW RILEY
Go.

WAYNE
Fifteen-two and a pair, for four.

WIDOW RILEY
A run for three and a pair, for five, with the Jack.

WAYNE
Cripes! You're a sharp one!

WIDOW RILEY
Ha! All in fun, Wayne.

WAYNE
If you say so.
(moves the pegs)

WIDOW RILEY
Did you see Marie this morning? She's doing better.

WAYNE
I popped my head in. She said Joe would be coming down to give me a hand with the haying.

WIDOW RILEY
She was so depressed lately, I was getting worried but it seems like the better weather is helping.

WAYNE
That rain was no help for the hay, I can tell ya'. Barely getting itself up off the ground, after that string of storms.

WIDOW RILEY

Is Maeve working today?

WAYNE
I don't know, not that she'd tell me. You, more like.

WIDOW RILEY
I was just wondering if she started working Saturdays yet.

WAYNE
Oh, she did mention something about that, now that you say it. Now, I've got to finish up here and get back out at 'er, before the heat gets too hard.

WIDOW RILEY
And Joe Hair is working out for you?

WAYNE
I will say it is a help to have an extra set of strong hands. He's not half-bad, I'll say, but that Tyler Bloodworth fella has got farming in his blood. I don't know how it's going with him and Maeve but I never knew the Flatheads to be real farmers. But by god, he's one.

WIDOW RILEY
Oh!

WAYNE
Why, I rode up by Plentywood with him to his Pa's place, and that's quite a spread. Him and his two sons have got the lines straight and square corners, I tell ya.

WIDOW RILEY
What is his father like? Did you talk to him?

WAYNE
I did. Old-time rancher-fella, but a smile a mile-wide, proud of his sons. Out of the three, I'd put Tyler at the top of the pile. Smarter and careful with his hands.

WIDOW RILEY
Did he talk about the baseball tryouts?

WAYNE
Not to me, but Maeve said he never took to the Cities, and the

crowds. Going up to see his old man, I can see why. Plenty of space up there.

WIDOW RILEY
Right.

WAYNE
Now you hung one on me here, but I'll get it back later.
(gets up)

WIDOW RILEY
Is that a promise?

WAYNE
Oh, now, you...

Wayne leans down and kisses Widow Riley.

Maeve comes in through the front door, holding an envelope.

MAEVE
You'll never guess what I've got?

WAYNE
Looks like a letter.

MAEVE
From Josie!

WAYNE
Have you now?

WIDOW RILEY
Oh! Did that come today?

MAEVE
I came through the post office and it was there.

WAYNE
Well, open her up, let's see.

MAEVE
(opens letter)
Oh, hey! Here is a picture!

She hands the picture to Widow Riley. It is a snapshot of Josephine outside in Montreal, in front of a big church. She is smiling and wearing an 'art-y' outfit.

WIDOW RILEY
Oh! Look at that. She's got a beret!

WAYNE
Roy G. Biv! Cripes, isn't that something!

MAEVE
Here, listen. She says,

JOSEPHINE
Greetings Montana from Montreal! I hope you are all doing well back home. I am busy with art classes and seeing the sights here. It's so different here but I am training myself to see with my artistic vision.

The city is beautiful and I have a small apartment. I pinned my picture of Dad up on the wall in my room so I can always remember you guys.

I got a letter from Marie and she says the baby Roy is doing really well. That's great! I hope she is doing OK now.

Tell Maeve that she's got to save up some money and come out here for two-weeks at my term break in the start of September. She's got to see all the gorgeous people here.

I want her to meet my friend Julie. We've been best friends since we arrived. She's from Saskatoon so we really get each other. She is working on making a set of full-sized buffalo out of blue paper-mâché. It's the funniest thing I've ever seen and the people here just can't get enough of it.

Tell Missus Riley that I miss her tons. I really had to lean on her when Uncle Reuben died and Marie moved back home. Tell her I love her.

Sorry for the rambling letter. I should close. Just want to tell Daddy I love him too.

xoxoxo! J.

WAYNE
(choked up)
Well, can you beat that?

MAEVE
Can I go, Daddy? Can I go to Montreal? Missus Riley?

WAYNE
Well, sure, I suppose it would be good for you to see the world some.
Maybe the Widow Riley should go too, go back East to see things
again.

MAEVE
Oh my, that would be wonderful! We could be travelling sisters.
Riding the rails!

WAYNE
Maybe put pen-to-paper and tell her you want the details.

MAEVE
Oh what fun!

Maeve exits out the door and heads into the other house.

WAYNE
Can you beat that?

WIDOW RILEY
But Wayne, if I take Maeve to Montreal, it will just be you in the
house and Marie and Roy next door. Won't that be lonely for you?

WAYNE
Well, Marie was telling me that Joe Hair's mother wants Marie to
bring little Roy up to the rez for a stay. Says they want to be sure Roy
grows up to know his people. Maybe that would be a swell time for
them to get to know little Roy.

WIDOW RILEY
And leave you all by yourself? I couldn't do that, leave you here all

alone.

WAYNE
It'd only be a couple weeks and I'm a big boy. I can handle myself, I should say. Why, I'm thinking about how quiet it might finally be, without my three hens clucking all the time. A fella could get a little rest at last.

WIDOW RILEY
But the bed gets cold at night.

WAYNE
Well, not any more. So that'll be the lure to get you back here, so you don't just stay out East.

WIDOW RILEY
I might need some more persuading...

WAYNE
Ah, all right. Come here, you.

Widow Riley stands up. Wayne takes her in his arms and they kiss in a long, passionate embrace.

WIDOW RILEY
Well, now...

WAYNE
That's gonna have to hold ya. I've got to get to haying, before heat grips it.

WIDOW RILEY
Oh, the heat. Hurry back.

WAYNE
The Hair boy is coming so, more hands make short work.

Wayne exits out the door.

Widow Riley packs up the card game and pegs. She straightens the items on the table and sits down with a cup of coffee.

She looks around, alone in the place.

WIDOW RILEY
(to herself)
And just like that, the world changes.

<u>END</u>

ART SCHOOL DRAMA

RICK REGAN

2021

EXT. MONTREAL LATE SPRING - DAY

Josephine is walking down a leafy sidewalk in Montreal. It is the end of May 1960. She is in her last year of art college. She is wearing chic casual clothes and a beret that suggests a Beatnik influence. She is carrying a bouquet of flowers as she heads from her apartment to the art studio.

On the sidewalk, heading the opposite direction is a group of nuns in the old-style full-habit and long dresses. One young nun looks at Josephine as they pass. Josephine looks at her and stops, then swivels around catching up with the nuns. She taps the young one on the shoulder. She stops and looks at Josephine.

JOSEPHINE
Here! For you.

She pulls one of the tulip stems out of her bouquet and gives it to the young nun. The sisters have a vow of silence. The young nun puts her finger to her lips, indicating quiet. The young nun takes the flower and just smiles and nods. They go on their way. An older nun glowers over her shoulder, disapproving of how Josephine is dressed.

JOSEPHINE
Good day, Sisters!

Josephine goes up the granite steps into the art studio.

INT. ART STUDIO - DAY

The studio is a big loft area, like a basketball court with a big open space. Inside there are areas where different young people, artists, are working on their Finals Project. There is a big block of stone with a man chiseling out a figure. There is a welder putting together big pieces of metal which hang by chains from a low crane. Julie, Josephine's friend, is putting paper mâché over metal frameworks of bison shapes.

JULIE
Hey Josie! Whatcha got?

JOSEPHINE
I picked up a bunch from the guy at the corner. It just reminds me of home to see something pretty.

Josephine goes to her station, with her bench and puts the flowers in a hand-thrown clay pot, from her first year ceramics class. There is a jug of water that she uses for the clay and she pours some into the pot for the flowers.

JULIE
Pretty!

JOSEPHINE
How are you coming along? Are you going to be ready by the end of term?

JULIE
We've got six weeks and I'm almost done. I might take a trip to Niagara Falls 'cause I'll have a week to spare.

JOSEPHINE
I've never seen the falls.

JULIE
You should get out more.

JOSEPHINE
Poor student, you know!

JULIE
You and me both, sister!

They both laugh.

JOSEPHINE
Are they all going to be blue?

JULIE
Well, they are a family, soooo.... Yeah.

JOSEPHINE
I'm just saying, you could make red ones or, I don't know, green ones, yellow even.

JULIE
Like teams, with jerseys?

JOSEPHINE
Maybe?

166

JULIE
No. Blue.

JOSEPHINE
Ok, Ok. Just a suggestion.

JULIE
How about you? Are you going to paint your guy red and yellow?

JOSEPHINE
Listen, I go to casting the bronze next week. It's kind of a one-shot deal. I'm just hoping it comes out in reasonable shape. I'm not going to worry about painting him.

JULIE
It's not all going to be cast in one piece?

JOSEPHINE
No, it goes in sections, but I have to get the face right. He was my father.

Gerard Fontainebleau, the seniors' instructor and studio manager, approaches, evaluating everyone's progress.

FONTAINEBLEAU
(Looking at the large figure)
Josie, I like what you are doing here. Tell me about the pose, with the arms out.

JOSEPHINE
He's throwing a spear. Hunting.

FONTAINEBLEAU
Do you have a spear?

JOSEPHINE
Not yet. I'm making one from a pattern, a Blackfeet spear.

FONTAINEBLEAU
Why Blackfeet? Where were they?

JOSEPHINE
They are on a reservation, in Montana.

FONTAINEBLEAU
They are still around? I thought they were all gone now.

JOSEPHINE
We're still here.

JULIE
Here? Even in Quebec?

JOSEPHINE
Well it's different people here but sure, natives are still here.

JULIE
So is this a protest piece, against the treatment of the Indians by the Americans?

JOSEPHINE
No. It's just my dad. He was full-blood Blackfeet.

FONTAINEBLEAU
But does he hunt with a spear, your father?

JOSEPHINE
He died when I was little. Car wreck.

FONTAINEBLEAU
So this is an idealized representation of the Native Man, adapted to the natural world but out of cycle with the modern world. Very good. I like it. Will you be ready for casting next week?

JOSEPHINE
I'll be ready. I'm going to have to be ready.

FONTAINEBLEAU
Quite right. And Ms. Hathaway, how are the buffalo?

JOSEPHINE
Bison. Good. I'm almost done. I just have a few more to paint.

FONTAINEBLEAU
(Skeptical)
All blue? Hmmm?

JULIE

(Unsure)
Yeah. All blue. They have all been blue.

FONTAINEBLEAU
Would you humor me and make a red one?

JULIE
Sir? I guess I could...

FONTAINEBLEAU
I'm just thinking that I want you to look deeper at your figures. You have a blank canvas, albeit bison-shaped, and the opportunity to introduce contrast, tension and drama to the collection. If you made them unique, people would see each one as an individual, instead of just glossing by the herd.

JULIE
You mean... like, stripes or something?

FONTAINEBLEAU
What about symbols? Or the cave painting figures, you know the ones, of the man hunting the mammoths? Or an American flag, HA! Or a hammer and sickle, or, or, I don't know. Just look and think a little harder. A blue herd is nice. But do you want to be just nice? What if you made the viewer stop and mutter under his breath, *what the hell is that?*

JOSEPHINE
Or a Canadian flag.

FONTAINEBLEAU
Oh my!

JULIE
(Flustered)
Ok. Ok. Let me think about it.

FONTAINEBLEAU
Yes, very good. Carry on.

Fontainebleau moves on to other students.

JULIE

Thanks for nothing. A Canadian flag, sheesh!

JOSEPHINE
Or the province flags. One each. You could have a Saskatoon flag bison.

JULIE
I don't have that many bison!

JOSEPHINE
Alright, calm down. Do whatever you want.

JULIE
Thanks. If I have your permission, I will.

JOSEPHINE
(Teasing)
You're a lunatic. They ought to lock you up.

JULIE
I'm going to lock you up, with this hammer and sickle.
(she waves her fist at Josie)

JOSEPHINE
Ha, ha! Alright, get back to work.

They both laugh and Josephine looks intently at her figure. She measures and carves with clay tools.

EXT. SIDEWALK NEAR UN*IVERSITEE DES QUEBEC AU MONTREAL (UQ*M) - EVENING

UQM has big, institutional style concrete buildings, much different from the Academy du Beaux Arts, the art college.

Julie and Josephine Webster are following groups of people down the busy sidewalk. It feels much bigger and important here.

They approach a blocky building with glary lights in the lobby.

JOSEPHINE
Is this it?

JULIE

(To a male student passer-by)
Excuse me. Can you help us?

JEAN-LUC
Ou *est la?*

JULIE
I'm sorry. An*glaise, s'il vous plais?*

JEAN-LUC
(Dismissive)
Ah, oui. What do you want, English?

JULIE
I'm looking for Granville Tower two. Is this it?

JEAN-LUC
(Points at the sign)
C'est ca. This is it.

JULIE
Thank you. Me*rci!*

JEAN-LUC
(Turns away)
Go home, English.

JOSEPHINE
Hmmph!

JULIE
Let's go.

INT STUDENT HOUSING BUILDING - SAME TIME

Josie and Julie go in and find their way to a common room on the fourth floor. It is a casual party, with bottles of beer and some French jazz playing. Lots of student types in clusters in the big space.

Josie finds Otto and his friends in a group, very animated talking.

NORMAN
(To the group)
Yo*u can't tell me that the petit bourgeoisie h*ave any interest in

171

helping the masses.   It's just not in their interests.

OTTO
Of course it's in their interests. If the peasants revolt, the rich go to the guillotine. Heads on pikes. Better to give them bread and circus.

NORMAN
The geo-political power centers run on the fuel of the poor, like logs fed to a steam engine. The progress re*quires e*xploitation.

EDDIE
That's crap. This is not the Eighteenth Century. There has not been a guillotine incident in North America since, what, *Richard l*ost at the Maple Leafs!

Th*ey all laugh at this hockey reference, of Montreal losing to Toronto.*

JOSEPHINE
(Butting in)
Otto. This is my friend Julie.

JULIE
(Awkward)
We do art together.

EDDIE
God bless the artists!

NORMAN
(Noticing the pretty women)
Here, here!
(raises beer bottles)

OTTO
So you guys just get here? What do you think?

JOSEPHINE
You guys throw a great party.

OTTO
We're just gassing around. Everybody goes to one econ lecture and thinks he's Prime Minister.

NORMAN
Hey, you guys coming to the rally tomorrow?

JULIE
What rally? What's it for?

EDDIE
Not what. It's who. Jean Lesage is giving a speech at UQM tomorrow afternoon. He's the Liberal running for Prime Minister of Quebec province. We're part of the Union Nationale protest. This guy thinks he can turn Quebec into some socialist paradise.

OTTO
But he's backed by the Soviets. This is all KGB meddling in our elections.

NORMAN
We're calling his bluff! Let everybody know that he's a stooge for the Commies.

EDDIE
He wants to turn the province into Red China. And you see how well that's going!

OTTO
If you want, you can join our action-front, spreading the word about this twisted *realpolitik.*

JULIE
Will it be fun?

EDDIE
Well have some signs and banners. And we'll have a couple of cases of beer, if that helps.

JULIE
Now you are talking my downtrodden language!

OTTO
(Hearing music)
Come on, Jo! Let's dance!

Josephine and Otto move to an area where people are dancing. Eddie and Julie grab hands and go to dance.

Scene of young people dancing, cool swing jazz playing. A fun night in Montreal.

EXT. LARGE GRASSY QUAD - SATURDAY MID-MORNING

There are hundreds of people milling around. Some in Quebec Liberal Party (QPL) sashes. Others in Partie Nationale straw boater hats. Groups gather and some are chanting.

A big stage is set up at one end and a student government person is giving a speech through a loudspeaker.

Josie and Julie arrive at the Quad, looking for Otto and the boys. They see the Nationale banner and they head over.

OTTO
You made it!

JOSEPHINE
Technically I'm an American.

JULIE
And technically I'm from Alberta.

NORMAN
But you can wear the hats!

Both Julie and Josephine take white straw boater hats, with a banner that says "Conservative!" across the front with a red, white and blue ribbon. They each admire how cute they look in the hats.

EDDIE
The commie is up next.

They hear the crowd start to cheer.

JULIE
I want to get a better view. You can't hear anything way over here.

JOSEPHINE
Let's get closer. We'll be back.

Julie and Josephine cross the green grass of the quad and fall in with the people in the crowd.

EXT. BEHIND THE STAGE - SAME TIME

Jean Lesage is with his campaign manager and other handlers. They check his tie, smooth his jacket and they discuss the speech. Finally they get the signal and Lesage moves to front of the stage, behind a microphone stand.

LESAGE
Good afternoon, friends. Good afternoon, people of Quebec. Bon Jour, Montréalais!
I am Jean Lesage. (pause, wait for applause)
Thank you.

I am here today to ask you to vote for me in two weeks.
But I know that to get to be the Prime Minister of Quebec, I cannot just ask for your vote. I have to earn it. I have to earn your hope. I have to earn your optimism for the future.

Before I tell you about the plans of the Quebec Liberal Party, I want to remind everyone about the plans of the conservative Union Nationale Party. They call themselves conservatives because they don't want things to change. Don't want to upset the old order. Don't want to change the status quo.

But the status quo is that over half of French Canadians in the province of Quebec live below the national poverty line. But the conservatives don't want that to change, while the majority lives in poverty with little opportunity.

The status quo is that less than fifteen percent of the economy of Quebec belongs to the people of Quebec. American mining companies haul out Quebec iron to American steel mills. Ontario paper companies haul out Quebec lumber from Quebec forests. Power plants, chemicals, agricultural products -food- all hauled away to Ontario or Ohio, only to sell it back to poor French Canadians. But the conservatives don't want that to change.

(Julie and Josephine take off their Conservative hats.)

The status quo is that less than twenty percent of French Canadians graduate from high school, the lowest number in the nation. Is that because the schools are run by the Church? Is it because schools are not in French at all? Is it because they stress Latin grammar, instead of science and engineering? And many of our students leave. They go to places that are engaged in the modern economy.   But the conservatives don't want to upset the status quo.

And the status quo is that our lives, our government, our schools and our economy are not decided in French Canada but in Ottawa, by English Canada. And the conservatives don't want to make any changes.

Il faut que ça change. Things have to change. Things have to change! Say it with me, Things have to change!

That's right. Maîtres chez nous. You know what this means? We must be the master in our own house.

Think of it. The people of Quebec making plans for the people of Quebec. And here, at University Quebec des Montreal, you are the future of our country. You are the Canadians we need, right here in Montreal. Not New York or Paris or Hong Kong. Here.

If you vote for the Liberal Party, we can change Quebec. We will change Quebec. This is Nineteen Sixty, not Sixteen-Sixty. After three hundred   years of the old-world rules, we are on the edge of the revolution; social, economic and political revolution in Quebec. Things have to change.

So vote for your future. Vote for our future. Vote for Quebec. Vote Liberal on June twenty-second. Vote Lesage!
Thank you! Thank you!

The crowd cheers and chants, "Lib-er-al! Lib-er-al! Lib-er-al!"

EXT. NATIONALE BOOTH - AFTER THE SPEECH

OTTO
(Yelling)
Comm-u-nist! Comm-u-nist! Comm-u-nist!

EDDIE
K-G-B! K-G-B! K-G-B!

NORMAN
Once again the Liberal candidate wants to hand out cookies and cake!
Everybody gets cookies! Everybody gets cake! But wait until you see
your tax bill. But you won't even see it! They'll just take it out of your
pay. Like you won't notice! Forget this nonsense, vote Conservative!

*Josephine and Julie approach. They look at the conservatives mocking
and chanting. They look at each other and turn to go. Julie throws the
hat in the air. Josephine keeps the hat but rips off the Conservative!
ribbon. They head across the quad, going back to 'their' side of town,
with the art college. From the crowd they hear a voice. It is the student
who they asked directions from the night before.*

JEAN-LUC
EH! Eh! Hey, English!

They stop, not recognizing the handsome young man.

JOSEPHINE
Hello? Yes?

Approaching them.

JEAN-LUC
You are the English. I saw you last night. You were going to the
Granville.

JULIE
Oh, yes. You were so rude to us. "An*glaise, go home!"*

JEAN-LUC
I apologize. I was rude. I am sorry. Are you leaving?

JOSEPHINE
We were meeting some boys here...

JULIE
But they are Conservatives. So, you know.

JEAN-LUC

Only the English would be Conservatives here. Come on, I'm with some friends. And I wanted to see you again.

They follow Jean-Luc to the edge of the quad, where a group of UQM students are standing around, smoking. There are some people on a blanket with a picnic. They are French.

ST. ANN
(Looking up from the blanket)
Oh, hello. You must be the girl.

JOSEPHINE
The girl?

ST. ANN
Please, sit down. This is Esmeralda. Sh*e's a gypsy!*

Josephine and Julie sit down with Louisa St. Ann and Esmeralda.

JOSEPHINE
What did you mean, the girl?

ESMERALDA
It was all Jean-Luc could talk about last night.

ST. ANN
He said he bumped into these two English girls and he couldn't stop thinking about them.

ESMERALDA
Or talking about you.

ST. ANN
So I said that you would probably be here today, so we should make a picnic and wait for you to appear.

ESMERALDA
But I told him, he had to go and look for you, or else your fortunes would never cross. And he did.

ST. ANN
And now you are here.

All four women look at Jean-Luc.

JEAN-LUC
I didn't think you would be hanging out with the Conservatives though...

JULIE
Who was that guy, the one that made the speech?

ST. ANN
That was Lesage. He's running for Prime Minister of Quebec province. The election is next month.

JEAN-LUC
But he'll never win. There are too many power people, in high-positions, you know, who don't want him to win. He wants to take away their money.

JOSEPHINE
Can he do that?

JEAN-LUC
Maybe. But he has to get elected first, and that's not likely. It's like he said, most people are poor and, especially up north, a lot of people can't even read. People get told where to mark on the ballot, by the shop foreman or the head guy at the mine. And things never change.

JOSEPHINE
It's like that on the *res* sometimes. Poor, neglected people who can't write enough to spell their names. Then we wonder why the Indians are still so poor.

ESMERALDA
The rez?

JOSEPHINE
I'm American, and half-Indian. Some of my family lived on the reservation in Montana. Do you know where that is?

JEAN-LUC
Yeah, sure. Down south and out west. Cowboys and Indians.

JOSEPHINE
Well... there are still Indians there, but not many real cowboys.

ESMERALDA
And you in Montreal? It's a long way.

JULIE
Academy des Beaux Arts.

ESMERALDA
You're artists?! I love it!

JOSEPHINE
Julie, here, makes huge, life-sized bison.

JULIE
And Josephine here, makes bronze figures. We have a showcase coming up in a few weeks. You should come.

ST. ANN
I thought you were UQM students, but art college. Wow!

ESMERALDA
Buffalo in Montreal! I love it.

JULIE
My instructor wants me to paint symbols and colors on them. I want to keep them as a family, in blue.

ST. ANN
Blue, for Quebec!

JULIE
He wants a red one.

ALL
He *must be English! Ha-ha-ha!*

JULIE
(Looks, puzzled)

JEAN-LUC
It is that red is the typical color for the English who want the French to go back to France. But we've been here longer than the English even.

JOSEPHINE

But not as long as the Indians...

JEAN-LUC
That's true but do you know the story of Quito?

JOSEPHINE
Quito? No.

JEAN-LUC
Quito was a slave. Well, Esmeralda, you tell it better than me.

ESMERALDA
Yes, yes. Quito. It was a long time a go. With Champlain and the Algonquin. You know the Algonquin?

JOSEPHINE
Actually, yes, I do. One of the boys in the Indian Society is Algo. Freddie. He says his people are from further up, like, north.

ESMERALDA
Oh! I see. It's just, well, it is legend. And nobody actually knows any Indians. But, maybe, you do. It makes the story, um, hard.

JOSEPHINE
It's like that sometimes.   Do you want to tell the story or are you afraid now?

ESMERALDA
Maybe afraid.

JOSEPHINE
Then let me tell you a story.

JEAN-LUC
No, let her finish. She tells the good version of Quito.

JOSEPHINE
Maybe we keep Quito for another time. Julie, let's go.

ESMERALDA
Wait. Hold on. It is a simple story. Quito is a boy but his family gets captured in a raid. Quito is made to be a slave of the French lieutenant. But he knows the land and he feeds the Frenchman slugs,

so he dies. But Quito is caught so they kill him. That's the story.

JOSEPHINE
Is that supposed to be funny?

JEAN-LUC
No! Not when she tells it like that! The parents say to the children that Quito will come for them if they are naughty. Quito will poison them if they do not eat their supper. It's a nice story.

JOSEPHINE
No. It's not. It's awful and I hate you. Do not follow me. Good bye.

JULIE
Let's go.

Julie and Josephine get up and head across the grassy quad, among all the people milling around on the beautiful spring day.

INT. BRONZE CASTING STUDIO - DAY

Josephine is watching as the cauldron of molten bronze is poured into her mold.   Using the lost-wax method, the bronze is poured into a sand mold, with wax melting from the hot metal.

There are several other students in line, each with their own wax & sand molds for casting bronze.

JULIE
Is it your turn?

Julie is with Josephine, watching the whole process but they are well back from the molten metal because of the danger. At a safe distance, the artists and friends are arranged on bleachers.

Jean-Luc comes in the rear door, but he is not seen by Josephine or Julie.

JULIE
Is that one yours?

JOSEPHINE
No, I'm two-down. See how the man is filling the mold, so slowly?

JULIE
Yeah.

JOSEPHINE
It's because it could crack, and break apart.

JULIE
Ouch!

JOSEPHINE
If the mold is broken, well that's bad, but the real issue is hot liquid metal flowing over the floor. That's why we're up here.

JEAN-LUC
(Climbing the bleachers)
Did I miss it?

JOSEPHINE
You?

JEAN-LUC
Yes! I wanted to see the casting. Like Rodin!

JOSEPHINE
Not like Rodin. August Rodin was a genius. This is just a senior project.

JEAN-LUC
Maybe you are a genius too!

JOSEPHINE
Jean-Luc, why are you here?

JEAN-LUC
I cannot live without you.

JOSEPHINE
You are a fool.

JEAN-LUC
I am a fool, in love with an English. I am ruled by my heart! What can I do? You make me a slave to my passion.

JULIE

Jean-Luc, did you come here by bicycle?

JEAN-LUC
No, I took the Society auto-bus.

JULIE
Then you have return ticket. So you should go home!

JEAN-LUC
I do not understand you, English. You are beautiful. You are intelligent. But you have no philosophy of love. Remarkable!

JOSEPHINE
What do you mean? Like Aristotle?

JEAN-LUC
No, like Descartes. Rousseau. We think, but we also feel. That is separate from thinking. And we should think, think!, about what we feel. Then we can decide if we should ruled by our reason, or by our passion.

JOSEPHINE
So what does that mean for me?

JEAN-LUC
It means that I saw you and I cannot forget you. I think you are beautiful. I think you are intelligent. And I think your casting is up next.

JOSEPHINE
Oh my! Yes, that's me.

They all watch as the bronze is poured into the sand mold. As the flow continues, a glowing gap appears on the side, creeping up the mold. Liquid bronze flows out of the gaps and   cracks, but the mold does not break. Finally the pouring finishes and the cauldron moves on to the next mold

Josephine collapses into crying.

JEAN-LUC
It's OK! It's OK. The mold did not break.

JULIE
You can fix it! Let it cool and you can fix it.

JOSEPHINE
(Jagged crying)
It's never going to be right! They won't let me graduate! They are
going to send me back to Montana!

JEAN-LUC
(Hugging her)
It's OK. It's alright. Like she said, let it cool. We can fix it in the
morning. Come on.

*Jean-Luc leads Josephine down the bleachers, heading towards the back
door. Julie gets up to go with them but Jean-Lug raises his hand, open
palm to her, to signal 'stay there'. Julie sits down.*

*Jean-Luc and Josephine walk through the streets of Montreal, it might be
raining, and they duck under cover of awnings when the downpour
comes.*

INT. JEAN-LUC'S APARTMENT - LATER

*They end up at his apartment, in the Jewish Quarter, with deli's,
bakeries, and coffee shops around every corner. It is a modest but
functioning neighborhood. The apartment is upstairs, above a sporting
goods/hockey equipment store.*

Jean-Luc puts a hotplate on, to heat some water for tea/coffee.

JOSEPHINE
I can't believe my whole year has gone to pieces.

JEAN-LUC
(Pours a French-press coffee)
Did it, though?

JOSEPHINE
Yes! You saw it. The thing is in pieces.

JEAN-LUC
But the one thing is not the measure of your art, your progress.

185

JOSEPHINE
Yes, it is! That is what I get the grade on.

JEAN-LUC
But you don't need the grade. You are an artist.

JOSEPHINE
I'm not an artist until they say I am an artist. That's how it works.

JEAN-LUC
Then you are right. You are not an artist. My mistake.

JOSEPHINE
What do you mean? Why do you say it like that?

JEAN-LUC
No, no. You are right.

JOSEPHINE
What?

JEAN-LUC
If you need their approval, their certification, to say that you are an artist, then you are not an artist. You are an amateur, a dilettante.

JOSEPHINE
I am not a dilettante!

JEAN-LUC
Then what are you? A shop girl? A grocery store clerk?

JOSEPHINE
How did you know I worked in a grocery store?

JEAN-LUC
Lucky guess.

JOSEPHINE
No. I need the certification so that I have the backing of the,....., the...

JEAN-LUC
Official people?

JOSEPHINE

Yes! I need the backing of the official art world.

JEAN-LUC
Then you are merely an illustrator. You should work at the magazine, Montreal Anglaise! Or is it, Montana Today?

JOSEPHINE
I'm not going back there.

JEAN-LUC
But you are not an artist, if you must have their approval. Have you learned nothing from them? Have they not shown you the philosophical dialogue, the debate of art? I mean, Rodin, he was responding to the Greeks, the Romans. He was the modern artist. But who are you?

JOSEPHINE
Why are you saying this? I want to go home. How do I get home?

JEAN-LUC
You should lie down.

JOSEPHINE
I'm not lying down, with you.

JEAN-LUC
Not with me. Not now. Just rest. I will sit here and sip coffee, and look at the light through the window. I just want you to rest.

JOSEPHINE
I will rest when I'm dead!

She *gets up to go.*

Jean-Luc advances and grabs her. He puts his arms around her and kisses her.

JOSEPHINE
Get away from me!

She pulls away.

JEAN-LUC
I'm sorry.

Josephine pulls herself away from him. She moves to sit on the bed. She sits and sighs.

JOSEPHINE
I just need to rest, someplace safe.

JEAN-LUC
You are safe. It is safe here. I won't touch you. Just lie down and relax.

Josephine lies back, closes her eyes and is quickly asleep.

Jean-Luc pours some more coffee and sits by the window, watching her and looking out at the street.

INT. BEAUX ARTS STUDIO - MORNING, NEXT DAY

Josephine's bronze casting is cooled and out of the sand. She is standing next to the misshapen hulk, looking for the figure she modeled.

FONTAINEBLEAU
(Approaches from behind)
Well, well. Hmm. Bit of a mess. Crack the mold?

JOSEPHINE
Some of it spilled.

FONTAINEBLEAU
(Inspecting)
These things happen. Hacksaw and grinding tool, you will be right the way there.

JOSEPHINE
(Incredulous)
Really?

FONTAINEBLEAU
Trim there, and you've got the arm. There, and you have the hip. Sand up the face some, and you are right on track. You are not far off. Well done!

JOSEPHINE
You mean that?

FONTAINEBLEAU
Some other castings are perfect. Some are not worth the sand for the mold. But as usual, each one represents the artistic talent of the sculptor. And yours, while rough and amateur, shows so much promise, of talent, intuition and, well, art, that I see this project and I wonder what you will do next. What is your next project?

JOSEPHINE
I'm still working on this one.

FONTAINEBLEAU
Of course, of course. It's just, well. It's just that you have talent. You have skill. But do you have your voice?

JOSEPHINE
Do I?

FONTAINEBLEAU
You are young. It is good that you master the skills. You can grow into your voice.

JOSEPHINE
Thank you, Mr. Fontainebleau.

FONTAINEBLEAU
Carry on.

We see Josephine wielding a grinding tool, cutting off flashing, smoothing rough edges.

INT. INSIDE A SMALL RESTAURANT NEAR UQM - EVENING

Otto and Josephine are sitting across from each other with plates of Italian food, with red-check table cloths.

OTTO
Jo?

JOSEPHINE
Hmm?

OTTO
Are you going to say anything, or do I have to do all the talking

189

tonight?

JOSEPHINE
What do you want me to say?

OTTO
How do you like the spaghetti? What happened with your art thing? What did you think of our protest at the rally last weekend? I don't know. Anything.

JOSEPHINE
The food is fine. My art thing came out OK. The protest was silly. And I think it might rain. There. Is that enough for you?

OTTO
Jo, what's the matter? I've never seen you like this. Is it something I said?

JOSEPHINE
I don't think this is a good idea. I should go home.

OTTO
Home? Jo, wait, there's something...

JOSEPHINE
What, Otto?

OTTO
There's something, some things, I think we should discuss.

JOSEPHINE
Go on.

OTTO
I mean we're both graduating. We have to think of the future. We've been together for almost a year. I guess I wanted to know if, well, you had real feelings for me.

JOSEPHINE
(Incredulous)
Wait, are you... is this... hold on, what's going on?

OTTO

Well, if you are going to be like that, I guess I have to just plunge in. Jo, what would you think of us getting an apartment this fall? And after that, maybe think about....being permanent?

JOSEPHINE
You mean, get married? To you?

OTTO
That's about the size of it, yes.

JOSEPHINE
(Moves to get up)
I don't think we should do this right now.

OTTO
Jo, honey! Sit down.

JOSEPHINE
(Standing, raising her voice)
No! I will not sit down. I'm going home.

OTTO
Honey, you're making a scene.

JOSEPHINE
(Loudly)
Thank you for dinner, Otto, but I am not going to get married, and certainly not to you.

OTTO
What are you talking about.

JOSEPHINE
Otto, I think I really saw you last weekend, with your friends, at the party and the rally. I really saw you, the real you. And I don't want to be with that person. You are arrogant, condescending and don't give a damn about my art. You want a pretty little wife, in a pretty little house, in a quiet neighborhood, while you go work at a big bank someplace. You want to be the big, important man, with your pretty wife waiting at home.

OTTO
Jo, sit down! For God sake! Get a hold of yourself!

JOSEPHINE
Well I don't want that. I don't want to be that. But don't worry! If you throw your wallet in any direction here, I'm sure there will be several good, solid Canadian girls just looking for Mister Right. You're a good catch, Otto! Just not for me. Goodbye!

All the heads in the restaurant swivel to watch her exit.

OTTO
(Stunned)
Check, please!

EXT. OUTSIDE JEAN-LUC'S APARTMENT BUILDING - NIGHT

Josephine has walked to Jean-Luc's building. She stands below his window, outside and call to him.

JOSEPHINE
Jean-Luc! Jean-Luc! Are you there?

Louisa St. Ann comes to the window and pulls the curtain aside.

ST. ANN
You are looking for Jean?

JOSEPHINE
Louisa, yes. Can I come up? I just broke up with my boyfriend.

ST. ANN
Oh my! Yes, of course! I will buzz you in.

Josephine goes up and into the student apartment building.

INT. INSIDE JEAN-LUC'S APARTMENT - NIGHT

JOSEPHINE
Louisa, what are you doing here?

ST. ANN
Josie, what are you doing here?

JOSEPHINE
I needed to be someplace but I didn't want to go home.

ST. ANN
And so you came here?

JOSEPHINE
I stormed out of a restaurant, a date with my boyfriend of a year, because I realized he was just another ordinary guy, in a sea of ordinary life. I didn't want that.

ST. ANN
But why here? Why Jean-Luc?

JOSEPHINE
I have been thinking about what he said after my art disaster. He seemed to understand, seemed to see me. Nobody ever did that for me.

ST. ANN
Oh yes. Jean-Luc will see you alright. He sees all the pretty girls.

JOSEPHINE
And you? Are you, and he...?

ST. ANN
On and off. I have known Jean-Luc since we were twelve. He is from my same town. We grew up together. I suppose we will get married eventually, but right now he wants to be with different girls. Today it's you.

JOSEPHINE
But he said he was crazy about me.

ST. ANN
Yes. He says that.

JOSEPHINE
I should go.

ST. ANN
You can stay if you want. He will be back soon. We were out of wine. We are working on the campaign action for the voting day, coming up.

JOSEPHINE

Lesage?

ST. ANN
We just volunteer with the campaign. Do you want to help?

JOSEPHINE
Actually, no. I don't want to get involved in politics.

ST. ANN
That's too bad. I think a campaign would be good for your art.

JOSEPHINE
Yeah, well, I'm going to go. Thank you for talking to me.

ST. ANN
Good night.

Josephine heads out and down the street.

INT. INSIDE THE BEAUX ARTS GALLERY - DAY - WEEKS LATER

It is three days after the election, Saturday June 25, 1960, clear, warm and bright. It is the day of the showcase of artists from the graduating class.

Each artist stands behind or near their work, to answer questions of the audience.

Josephine and Julie are placed next to each other, so that it looks like Josie's Native Man is hunting Julie's bison. The bison all have different colors, flags, symbols and markings.

A big press contingent is swelling in the gallery, with flashes going off and men talking into microphones.

JULIE
I can't believe all these people!

JOSEPHINE
Something is up. There is no way all this press is for us. Hey, here comes Fontainebleau!

FONTAINEBLEAU

Good morning, ladies. Everything looks good, I see.

JOSEPHINE
Why did you set them up like this, like he is hunting her bison?
Nobody else's is like that.

FONTAINEBLEAU
Julie, I love what you did with the bison. Swiss flag, American flag,
Quebec flag, and the zebra stripes, giraffe spots. Marvelous!
Excellent work!

JULIE
I realized that I had to break out of the conventional mold of realism,
and take a position in the symbolic context; creating, as you said,
tension and conflict.
(she winks at Josie)

FONTAINEBLEAU
(Delighted)
Ohhh! I couldn't have said it better myself. You have really stretched
the boundary of civil propriety.

JULIE
Well, uh, yeah. That's what I was going for.

FONTAINEBLEAU
And Josephine. The bronze figure is a revelation in primitive art. The
Native voice is not heard enough. The figure of the man with dignity
is a shocking expansion of the artistic landscape. Now, anything is
possible.

*The press swells around Josephine and Julia, while Fontainebleau scans
the crowd. Then, Fontainebleau sees Lesage, newly elected Prime
Minister of Quebec.*

FONTAINEBLEAU
Monsieur! Monsieur Premier!

LESAGE
Ah, Fortesque!

Lesage approaches Fontainebleau and the artists.

FONTAINEBLEAU
Premiere, I welcome you to Beaux Arts.

LESAGE
Ah, Fortesque, if I had known there were artistes such as these...
(stares at Julia)
I would have found my way so much earlier.

FONTAINEBLEAU
So, Miss Webster has a figure, native and brave.

LESAGE
Mighty hunter..

FONTAINEBLEAU
And Miss Hathaway has the bison of the plains.

LESAGE
I see. There is the give and take of the hunted and the hunter. So raw.
So alive.

FONTAINEBLEAU
Just so.

LESAGE
But the hunter will prevail. Like the badges on the buffalo, the
province doesn't matter when you are dead. Charge the hunter and
take a spear in the head.

*Lesage stands next to the buffalo with the Canada flag, while press
people take pictures and make notes.*

FONTAINEBLEAU
They are students.

LESAGE
(Hamming it up for the press)
You see the Native man? He is the Canadian! He is the man who
looks at the English world and says "Non!"
We look at the world of our French forefathers and, must we ask,
'How did you survive?' How did they maintain their dignity, in the
face of English oppression? Through strength. Through action. That
is our mandate for Quebec: Strength and Action!

FONTAINEBLEAU
I'd be glad to talk about it with you.

LESAGE
(To Josephine)
I'd like to know what you think. Bank of Montreal Hotel, room 232.
Come up after lunch.
(tosses her the key)

Lesage leaves, and the press follows.

Josephine pockets the key. Julie stares at her.

JULIE
What the hell was that? Did the Premier of Quebec just make a pass
at you?

JOSEPHINE
Maybe he just wants to talk about art.

JULIE
He wants to get inside your sweater, is what he wants!

JOSEPHINE
Maybe my prospects are looking up. It could be a good career move
to be involved with a famous politician.

FONTAINEBLEAU
(Approaches)
Give me the key.

JOSEPHINE
What key?

FONTAINEBLEAU
Just give it to me. I will not stand for a politician poaching our
students.

JOSEPHINE
We just graduated.

JULIE
We're not students anymore.

FONTAINEBLEAU
Just give me the key. I will deal with this matter myself.

JOSEPHINE
(Realizing Fontainebleau is gay)
You want him for yourself, don't you? Isn't that against the law?

FONTAINEBLEAU
Not for artists. Are you going to give me the key, or not.

JOSEPHINE
Not.

Josephine and Fontainebleau stare at each other, feeling the power shift between them.

FONTAINEBLEAU
Then I must warn you: do not start a fire that you cannot put out.

JOSEPHINE
I'm from Montana. I am familiar with wildfires. And how to put them out.

FONTAINEBLEAU
Miss Webster, you are talented, really gifted, as are you Miss Hathaway. It has been my honor to work with you both. Now you must excuse me.

Fontainebleau exits.

JULIE
What the hell was that?

JOSEPHINE
I don't know and I don't care. I am going to see the PM.

JULIE
AFTER lunch. Let's go eat.

JOSEPHINE
RIght. Food first.

EXT. SUNNY PARK OUTSIDE THE ACADEMY DES BEAUX ARTS - LATER

Julie and Josephine have baguette sandwiches with ham and butter, the popular Montreal street food, with Swiss cheese and mustard. They are sitting on a bench below a shady tree, watching all the people go by.

JOSEPHINE
This kind of feels like the end.

JULIE
It seems like there is a lot more to say.

JOSEPHINE
But here we are. We graduated and I broke up with Otto. And I finished my casting.

JULIE
What about Jean-Luc?

JOSEPHINE
Louisa says he's just playing the field. Whether that's true or not, I don't really care. I don't want to get into the middle of their world.

JULIE
Are you going to go back to Montana?

JOSEPHINE
Not if I can help it. Are you going to go back to Saskatoon?

JULIE
Not if I can help it!

JOSEPHINE
Let's get an apartment here. We can share.

JULIE
I was going to say that all along but I thought you were going to marry Otto.

JOSEPHINE
You thought that too?

JULIE

You didn't? Sweet child. Anybody could see that coming a mile away. He likes you and he's a good catch.

JOSEPHINE
He's a snob and a philistine. I didn't even realize a person could be both culturally lazy and be condescending about it in the same breath. I don't have any time to waste on Otto.

JULIE
But he wants to marry you.

JOSEPHINE
He'll marry the next thing that swishes by him in a skirt and some heels.

JULIE
Even if it's Fontainebleau?

JOSEPHINE
Ha! Ok, probably not him.

JULIE
(Laughs)
Did you see him swoon over Lesage? He was like a schoolgirl.

JOSEPHINE
I guess I never noticed it but it was there all along. Gosh, a pervert.

JULIE
But he knows art.

JOSEPHINE
What do you want to do now?

JULIE
Finish this sandwich and then let's us go get an apartment.

JOSEPHINE

(Coy)
Before or after my lovers' tryst with the new Prime Minister?

JULIE
You're not really going, are you?

JOSEPHINE
(Holds up the key)
I have to put on my big girl panties but I'm going.

JULIE
He just wants to use you. You know that, right?

JOSEPHINE
Julie, I see now that you are the only one for me. You have been there all along, you and me. We've got to stick together. But I want to have some fun and I want to get to the top.

JULIE
The top of what? The only thing climbing on top is that man climbing on top of you!

JOSEPHINE
The top of everything! And when the door opens, I'm going through it! Besides, it's not like me and Otto were holy saints. But I'm careful. My sister got pregnant from fooling around with a local boy, so I know I have to look out for myself.

JULIE
Oh, you're naughty!

JOSEPHINE
Jules, I was raised on a farm. I know what the bull wants. And you know what they say about Montreal?

JULIE
Good girls go to heaven. Bad girls come to Montreal!

JOSEPHINE
(Laughs)

I guess that's us!

JULIE
That's us!

JOSEPHINE
Ok, I'm going to go see lover-boy.

JULIE
Are you sure you want to?

JOSEPHINE
It's the next chapter, darling!

JULIE
Fly, girl, fly up to the sky.

JOSEPHINE
Julie?

JULIE
Yes?

JOSEPHINE
One last thing.

JULIE
What's that?

JOSEPHINE
Kiss me.

JULIE
What?

JOSEPHINE
Kiss me, before the moment is passed.

Julie leans in and Josephine kisses her. They hold the kiss for a moment and then separate.

JULIE
That was nice.

JOSEPHINE
You got butter on me. What will Lesage say?

JULIE
(Bursts laughing)
You're crazy!

JOSEPHINE
(Teasing)
I think you are mentally deranged!

JULIE
You're a nut-case!

JOSEPHINE
You're not all there, my dear!

JULIE
Go! Just go. Go see your hot new man. He is cute. Is
he married?

JOSEPHINE
Today, I don't care. I'll see you later.

Josephine gets up to go.

JULIE
Be careful, will you, for me?

JOSEPHINE
Yes, dear. Bye.

Josephine walks toward the Bank of Montreal Hotel.

JULIE
Don't get lost, little girl. Don't get mixed up in the big
city. I'll still be here, waiting.

She sits for a moment, watching Josephine, then gets up and walks the other
way, into the sunny afternoon.

<u>END</u>

Made in the USA
Middletown, DE
16 October 2023

40749181R00117